Holiday Flirts!
5 Romantic
Short Stories

Lisa Scott

CONTENTS

1 "Spooked By Love"   3

2 "Holiday Rush"   Pg #35
3 "Missing Christmas"   Pg #75
4 "Tingle All The Way"   Pg #100
5 "Giving Up Guys"   Pg #130
6 About the Author   Pg #169

"Spooked By Love"
by Lisa Scott

"Mommy, your tail's falling off," Chelsea said, as we stood on her friend's front porch, twenty minutes late for her Halloween party. She looked up at me with her halo and wings askew.

I straightened them and then checked my costume. Sure enough, my long black tail was coming unattached. I sighed and pulled it off. Duct tape was *not* good for everything, after all. Just one more thing my ex was wrong about—that and his stance on exercise videos as a suitable Valentine's gift.

I stuffed my tail in my purse. "Good thing I painted on whiskers, otherwise they might not know I'm a cat." I hadn't planned on dressing up for the party, but Chelsea had pouted long and hard enough to get me to do it. Faded yoga pants and a black turtleneck might not be the most creative ensemble, but I'm not exactly the sewing type. You work with what you've got, right?

"All the mommies will be dressed up. Daddy would do it," she'd said, stomping her foot. Since the divorce, Chelsea had been fine-tuning the art of playing me against my former husband. The truth was, my ex would not have dressed up. But Chelsea had seen me sad so often over the past few months, I'd decided to be a sport and wear a costume. I had to remind her Mommy could be fun, before all those memories of our good, happy times spent together were forgotten.

Two big eyes and a unicorn horn appeared in the window next to the door. Chelsea's friend, Danielle, let us in. "Come on! You're late."

Chelsea rolled her eyes. "Mommy's always late."

I couldn't argue; it was true.

"Come downstairs—everybody's here!" Grasping Chelsea's hand, she led us toward the sound of music and the tinkling laughter of little kids.

We followed her down to the basement, filled with

2

candy-crazed kindergartners chasing each other around the big, finished playroom. I scanned the room for the other adults and saw several women huddled around a table, casting curious glances my way. It didn't take long to realize they weren't in costume. In fact, they were wearing cute fall blazers, killer boots, and cuddly sweaters. They all looked very Mommy-chic; something I'd never been able to pull off.

I swallowed the lump in my throat and looked away from their smirks. Not only did I look unfashionable, I was the only guest over the age of five who was dressed up. Crossing my arms, I tried to blend into the corner. Maybe I could take my ears off and no one would notice. That's when I remembered the whiskers and pink nose on my face. *Perfect.*

"Watch out, I think they've got a dog upstairs."

I looked over at a man sitting at a table, holding a glass of cider and fighting back a grin. His brown eyes stood out against his green shirt. Nope, no costume on him, either.

I closed my eyes and forced a smile. "My daughter told me parents would be dressing up."

"Sounds like she played a little Halloween trick on you." He held out his hand. "Jeff Williams. Your daughter's in Mrs. Davison's class?"

I walked over and shook his hand. "I'm Marnie James, and yes, the little *angel* over there is my daughter, Chelsea." I pointed her out.

He laughed. "Well, the devil next to her is my son, Trey. They make a good pair. Say, where's your tail?"

I pulled it from my purse and held it up. "It hasn't been the best night."

He dismissed the idea with the wave of his big hand. "You're dressed up as a Manx cat. Very clever. But you look like you need a drink." He gestured to the table filled with sodas, cider, and juice. "Some milk, maybe?"

I rolled my eyes. "So, you *did* come to the party in

3

character—as a comedian?"

He crossed his arms. "Nope, I'm not funny, just funny looking."

But that wasn't true at all. He was very handsome *and* funny—the perfect combination. I snuck a peek at his left hand and didn't see a ring. It'd been a long time since a guy had caught my eye, and there I was, dressed as a cat. Not that I was looking. Nope, I had zero desire to date after fouling up my marriage so badly. I really hoped this guy wasn't single, too; I didn't need the temptation.

I flashed another look at his bare left hand. Maybe he was married, but he'd lost his wedding ring. Maybe it got caught on machinery at work and he couldn't wear it. Maybe he'd been robbed. *Yeah, that's it.* "So, it's just you and your son here?" I asked, having never figured out how to subtly inquire if a man was single.

"Nope, there's a whole room full of people here." He laughed and I noticed the cute dimples in his cheeks. "But if you're referring to my ex-wife, let's just say she would have come dressed as an evil harpy queen, and I don't see any of those here—at least not over the age of six. And you? Are you married?"

I shook my head. "No, I'm a single mom. Chelsea's dad wouldn't be caught dead dressed up at a Halloween party."

"Not even as a zombie?"

"Huh?"

"Caught dead—zombie?" He sighed, running his hand through his hair. "Don't worry, eight out of ten of my jokes work. The next one will be funny, I promise."

I grinned. "I look forward to it."

"Thank you, thank you very much, I'm here all night."

Good, I thought, surprising myself. I laughed nervously and adjusted my cat ears. "I feel so stupid being the only one dressed up. It's like I'm back in school and none of the cool girls will talk to me." I gestured to the mommies across the room. I recognized a few from morning drop-off, but again, I was usually late and never had much time to chat.

"Maybe they're allergic." He shrugged. "Don't feel bad. It just shows that you're a fun parent. They probably feel dumb that they didn't dress up, too. I wish I would've." He looked me up and down in my costume and I wondered what he thought. His eyes met mine. "Is your hair really that gorgeous red, or did you color it for the party?"

I knew I was blushing beneath my whiskers. "No, that's my real color. I hated it when I was growing up, but now I like it." Every time I went in for a haircut, I heard the same thing from the receptionist: "What a beautiful color! Please tell me you're not changing it?"

I always assured her no, and then she always asked me if it was real, like I'd never been there before.

Jeff and I chatted some more as we watched the kids play. They raced across the room with cotton balls on plastic spoons, trying not to drop them. They bobbed for apples and decorated pumpkins. They were having a great time; and so was I, even with my whiskers.

Chelsea scampered over. "Mommy, fix my wings!" I straightened her up and when she ran off, Jeff was gone. My heart sank. It had really seemed like we hit it off. But maybe he'd just felt sorry for me.

It was for the best, though. I couldn't imagine ever having the courage to date again. I'd thought it was the real thing with Bill. How could I trust my instincts now? The hurt of lost love was more painful than being alone.

The way I figured it, just like I wasn't meant to run a marathon, I wasn't destined for long-term love, either. It wasn't natural. Centuries ago, people died before they could get annoyed with one another. *We're living too long, that's the problem*, I often told myself. It was one theory, anyway. I had a few of them that I brought out from time to time to make myself feel better when chocolate didn't do the trick. My clothes had gone up two sizes since the divorce just to make the whole thing that much more fun.

The kids were lining up for a whack at the cheery pumpkin piñata, when someone tapped me on my shoulder. "There. Now you're not the only adult dressed up." Jeff stood in front of me, with candy taped to his pants.

I raised an eyebrow. "What are you supposed to be?"

His smile fell and his dimples disappeared. "Seriously, you can't tell?"

"Umm…" I shook my head, nibbling my lip.

Sighing, he pulled off one of the candies, and handed it to me.

"Smarties?" I asked, rolling the candy across my palm.

"I'm a smarty pants. Get it?" He swept a hand along the side of his body, showing off his impromptu look.

I covered my mouth to keep from laughing too hard.

He pretended to look offended, but burst out with a laugh. "Hey, I get an 'A' for effort, don't I?"

I nodded. "Absolutely."

"Good." He sat down across the table from me. "So, I'm invited to a grownup Halloween party next weekend. Would you like to come? We've already got fabulous costumes." He waggled his eyebrows.

I blew out a long breath. My heart was shouting 'yes,' but my brain stamped its foot 'no'—kind of like Chelsea often did. "I don't think so."

My brain usually won *that* fight—just like my daughter. But that's me—practical, pragmatic Marnie. My parents told me I'd rotate the toys I played with when I was two years old so I wouldn't wear them out. Little Baby Wet-'n-Sip got stashed away for a few days even though she was my favorite. I'd been denying myself pleasure from day one. Old habits dig in their heels over time.

Jeff snapped his fingers. "Wait, just a minute. I know what the problem is. I'll be right back." He dashed over to the big cauldron of candy and goodies set up on a banquet table, dug through the treats inside, and hurried back. He sat down and stared at me, all serious. Then he smiled, showing off neon-green vampire teeth. "Do you 'vant to go out 'vith me now?" he said, with a deep, sultry, Dracula accent.

I laughed so hard I thought I might hiccup. "Because you're wearing fake teeth?"

Frowning, he lost the accent. "I heard women are really into vampires these days." He shrugged. "Did my sister lie to me about that?"

My lips twitched into a smile. This guy could've been a new hot member of the Cullen family from *Twilight*, but I still wouldn't go out with him. "I'm sorry, not even the sexiest, pointiest, vampire teeth could tempt me."

He leaned across the table towards me, lowering his voice. "I'm a police officer. Are women into police officers these days? I've got the uniform and everything."

I giggled—and I am so not a giggler. "I'm sure plenty of women have a thing for police officers."

"But not you." Pulling out his fake teeth, he cocked his head. "My ex constantly reminds me how thick I am, but I thought conversation and laughter were an indication things were going well, and that it would be safe to propose getting together. Have the dating rules changed again?"

I sighed, twisting open the package of Smarties he'd given me. "No, you're doing quite well. You just picked the wrong girl. I'm not ready to get back in the dating game."

He looked at me and nodded. "I see. You're not just a cat, you're a scaredy cat."

I leaned back in my seat. "Hey, that's not fair. I'm a cautious cat. Who knows what a little curiosity could do to me at this stage in the game?" I popped a Smartie in my mouth and winced at the tangy taste.

His voice softened. "You haven't been divorced long, I take it?"

I shrugged. "Ten months."

He looked surprised. "And you haven't dated at all?"

I felt my body stiffen and shook my head. I stacked the round discs of candy on top of one another, concentrating on them instead of his chocolate-brown eyes.

"Have you ever heard the great advice I like to offer clumsy equestrians?"

I bristled. "This isn't just falling off a horse. This is like crashing a plane. Imploding a building by mistake." I flashed my hands in the air, mimicking an explosion. "I feel like that Valdez guy. I'm the captain of a ship who didn't have a clue how to drive the damn thing." And just like an oil spill, it'd take years to clean up. I knocked over my stack of candy and shrugged. "I can't risk that again."

With a satisfied look, he crossed his arms. "I think you were driving the wrong vehicle."

I rolled my eyes. "And let me guess, you're more suitable? A nice, fast, train?"

He sat back and looked offended. "I'm certainly not fast, I can assure you of that." He set his hand next to mine. "So, your ex broke your heart. He was a jerk. You're going to let him ruin the rest of your life?"

Pressing my eyes shut, I tried to hold back the tears, but my thick voice gave my emotions away. "I was the jerk. I ended things. He didn't cheat, he didn't drink— none of that. It just wasn't working. After being so sure he was the one, turns out I was wrong." I sniffed and looked up at him. "I don't know how people get the courage to try again. I guess you're right. I *am* a scaredy cat."

He leaned toward me. "Who says you have to get married again? I'm certainly not going to. But you can still have fun." He shrugged, like he was some financial guru offering stock advice on The Today Show.

I shook my head. "Then what's the point? It's just going to end up in a breakup instead. And that hurts, too."

"But there's no big mess. It's a huge difference. That's a lot of ridiculous pressure you're putting on yourself. You won't go out with someone unless you think it could end in a perfect, divorce-proof marriage?" He rolled his eyes, and I would have been annoyed if he hadn't looked so cute doing it.

I shifted in my seat. "It's not ridiculous, it's smart."

"What you need is a practice date." He took out a business card and wrote on the back. "Here. This is my cell number. If you decide you want to go to the party next weekend, let me know. It'll be fun; no crashing boats, no skittish horses, and no imploding buildings. Just a cat and a smarty-pants having a good time."

I smiled at him, even though I knew I wouldn't call. "Thanks."

If he was determined never to marry again and just out looking for fun, he was the last person I should be going out with. Even though he was funny. And friendly. And handsome—really handsome.

The party was breaking up, so I rounded up Chelsea, and found her battered wings lying on the floor, along with a huge bag of candy. "Let's go, kiddo." I needed to leave before I got sucked into those incredible eyes of his. Who knew a kids' Halloween party could be so scary for a single woman tucked in the corner with a hot stranger?

I hustled Chelsea out of there and got home to the comfort of my couch, hot tea, and fun-sized candy bars. They definitely did *not* provide the kind of fun I was longing for. They just left me with an unfamiliar twinge of regret and hope mingling in my chest.

And six hundred extra calories looking for a place to call home.

***

I dropped Chelsea off at Bill's apartment Saturday morning before work. I tried not to stare at him as he stood in his doorway. He'd taken up running since we'd divorced and shaved off his goatee, revealing the sharp, angled lines of his face. Why couldn't he have become a jiggly couch potato instead? Now he was hotter than ever. He'd moved on just fine without me. But attraction had never been our problem. Our problems were more along the lines of control and respect—two things he didn't like to give me very often. I couldn't forget that, no matter how good he looked.

"Be good for Daddy," I told Chelsea, kissing her head.

"I will." Chelsea ran inside with her Hello Kitty! suitcase and pink pillow, leaving me on the porch of his downstairs apartment. Bill had even been bitten by the entrepreneurial bug and had bought a duplex after we split, so he could use the upstairs rent to pay the mortgage.

Basically, my leaving was the best thing that'd ever happened to him.

He scratched the back of his head and yawned. "Hey, just wanted to give you a heads up that I'm going to introduce Chelsea to my girlfriend this weekend. I've been holding off until I knew it was serious."

I stepped back, my hand grazing my throat. "Oh. And it is? Serious?"

He nodded. "I like Pam. A lot."

I clenched my teeth. "Good. That's great. Really. Thanks for letting me know."

"Sure thing. I'll drop Chelsea off Sunday night. Do you want me to bring Pam so you can meet her? You know, since she'll be spending time with Chelsea?"

I gulped. *Oh, what fun.* "Sure. That's probably a good idea. But I'll pick up Chelsea." I didn't have the time to clean my place to make it meet-your-ex's-girlfriend worthy. If she saw the house now, she'd probably congratulate him on the divorce.

He shrugged. "Cool. Can you get her before dinner? Pam and I have reservations at that new Italian place in town."

"Yep." The only place close to Italian we'd ever gone was Domino's—for takeout. I turned and walked to my car, and thankfully I didn't cry until I pulled out of his driveway. He'd found a meet-the-daughter-worthy woman and I couldn't even envision my first post-divorce date.

I drove to work, and the familiar sense of dread filled my chest. It's hard to imagine working at a fruit orchard could be tough on a newly divorced woman, but it was. It had seemed like a good idea, but turned out to be torture. Every weekend in October they held a fall festival, and the place was jam-packed with kids and intact families, smiling daddies, and glowing mommies rubbing pregnant bellies rounder than the pumpkins we sold. Coming here each year was a holiday tradition for most families in the area.

Since I'd cried off most of my makeup on the ride over, I figured I'd take the pumpkin costume for the day. I could just paint my face orange and be done with it. All the employees at Gruber's Barn had to dress up for the fall festival. The teenaged girls who worked there always grabbed the cute costumes, like the sexy, purple witch outfit, or the mermaid with the ripped tail, fastened together with safety pins. Someone had been smart enough not to use duct tape—probably a woman.

I usually got stuck with the scarecrow or the clown, but I wasn't feeling funny enough today to pull that off. A bright orange pumpkin would suit me fine for my sad Saturday.

If that wasn't bad enough, since I was running a few minutes late, all the fun jobs were taken, too. Mindy and Trina—the teenaged cute-costume-stealers—were manning the helium-balloon tank and dunking-for-apples booth. The owner's son was wearing the pirate costume, handing out cider and candy, while Gayle, my only real friend at the place, wore the scarecrow costume while she manned the gift shop. She flapped a straw-filled glove at me as I walked by.

I ducked in the shop to say hello.

"Tell me about your wild Friday night," she said, smacking open a roll of dimes on the cash register drawer. Gayle was happily married and thought I should be living some swinging-single lifestyle so she could live vicariously.

"Kids' Halloween party. I was the only adult dressed up. Super fun." Then I thought of Jeff's contagious laugh. "I did meet a nice guy."

She raised her thick painted-on eyebrow. "Oh? Are you going out?"

I shook my head. "You know me. But he was funny and cute. A police officer. Jeff Williams."

Her eyes widened and a knowing grin appeared. "I know Officer Williams. Officer Hottie, as my friends like to call him. He went out with my friend, Lucy." She twisted her lips. "And Tara. She speeds when she's in his precinct, hoping he'll pull her over."

He's a player. "Well, he won't be going out with me." I jerked my thumb over my shoulder. "Off to pumpkin punishment."

She wrinkled her nose. "I'm so glad you're always late. I hate pumpkin duty."

I trudged off to the only assignment left. I was going to be in charge of pumpkin painting—always messy, never fun.

This day was certainly doing a number on my self-esteem. I stepped into the enormous costume, slathered orange paint on my face—adding eyes and a black frown—then slapped on my green cap. I waddled out to the picnic table in front of the huge pumpkin patch and sat down on the edge of the bench. Every kid who bought a pumpkin got to paint a little one and take it home for free. But the kids usually weren't happy with just one pumpkin, or they wanted colors we didn't have, or dropped them on the ground and cried when they got dirt and gravel on their wet paint.

Looking down at myself, I frowned. *No worries about meeting a guy in this costume.*

Jerry Gruber, the owner, came by with a wagon filled with little pumpkins for me. "I did some extra advertising this week, so this should be our busiest weekend ever."

"Yay!" I tried to sound enthusiastic. Gruber's wasn't my full time job. It was just a way to pick up a little extra cash for the holidays. I worked Monday through Friday as a receptionist at a hotel in town. My dream was to open a gift shop, but now with all the bills to pay on my own, that would never happen. At least if Bill had dumped me I could blame this all on him.

The only plus about the job was that Jerry let me sell my crafts there. That's how I'd found out about this part-time gig, anyway. I'd stopped by to see if he'd be interested in selling my fall wreaths and arrangements, and I saw that they were looking for someone to help out on Fall Fest weekends. Back in August it'd seemed like a good idea, and the money would help pay for all the craft supplies. I'd gone a little overboard after the divorce. Bill had always hated when I did crafts, moaning and complaining about all the supplies. So, I bought tons of supplies once he was gone; but the only thing that had hurt was my credit card balance.

If only I could show him some day it wasn't just a silly little hobby I "diddled around with," as he'd liked to say. Grumbling, I stood up and arranged the painting supplies.

The morning started off slowly until people started picking out and paying for their pumpkins. By noon, three different kids had started crying when it was time to leave, two had spilled paint, and another had thrown his pumpkin at his baby sister. Luckily, he didn't appear to have a future as a major league pitcher. I was fishing his pumpkin out of the garden behind me when I heard a familiar voice. "You had so much fun in the cat costume, you couldn't help yourself, could you?"

No, no, no. Looking at the apple orchard on the other side of the pumpkin patch, I thought about running for it. But I didn't like to run in general, and certainly not in a pumpkin costume. I sucked in a deep breath and turned to him. "Hello."

Jeff wasn't even trying to hide his grin.

"How did you know it was me?" I asked as calmly as I could.

"I spotted you from across the parking lot. No one has red hair like yours. It really stands out against the orange." He rubbed his chin as he checked me out in my orange glory. I'm sure my blush added to the whole burnished effect.

I patted my hair. "It's a nice touch, right?"

"Very nice." He pushed his son toward me. "Trey, say hello to Chelsea's mom."

He looked up from the caramel apple he was finishing. "Hi. Where's Chelsea?"

I smoothed the front of my pumpkin costume, as if that would help anything. "She's with her dad."

Licking his fingers, he nodded. "My dad's dropping me off at my mom's after this." He looked down and kicked a stone.

I caught Jeff's eye and we stared at each other, sharing a moment of sadness that divorce leaves in its wake.

Then Jeff rubbed his hands together, a devilish twinkle returning to his eyes. "How many costumes do you have for Halloween, anyway?"

I looked down at the reams of orange fabric billowing over me. "Oh, I can't claim this beauty. This belongs to Gruber's. Want to paint a pumpkin, Trey?"

"Sure." He settled at the picnic table and I set him up with supplies.

"This is where you work?"

"Only as a part time gig in the fall. Gotta make up extra money where I can, you know?" I set a small pumpkin in front of Trey.

Jeff picked it up. "This is kind of a reverse Cinderella thing. When do you switch from a pumpkin back into a woman? I'd really like to see you out of costume." One eyebrow raised.

I blushed, and he noticed. Then his cheeks reddened. "Well, not entirely out of costume... you know what I mean," he said quickly, faking a cough and setting the pumpkin down.

It was cute to see him flustered. "I'm done at five."

"Wanna catch dinner? I can pick you up after I drop off Trey."

My heart raced; from dread or lust, I wasn't sure. Either way, it scared me. "Most places don't allow pets or pumpkins."

"Right. Good thought. You could change and meet me somewhere, or I could pick you up."

I twisted my lips. It was strange to run into him two days in a row. Was this fate telling me something? I shook off the idea. I didn't believe in fate or feelings or intuition anymore. Not when mine had been one hundred percent wrong about Bill. I decided to marry him because I'd met him on the day I'd turned nineteen at a concert. I thought it was lucky—he agreed, and got lucky—and look how that'd turned out. Plus, "Officer Hottie" was probably just looking for a good time, too. So why bother starting anything?

I shook my head. "I don't think so. Being a pumpkin takes a lot out of a girl. But thanks."

His smile disappeared and he shrugged. "You've still got my number if you'd like to join me at the party next week."

"Right. Thanks." I adjusted the cap on my head as if I were wearing a couture outfit from that fancy store downtown, Sublime.

Luckily, a line was forming, so I had to turn my

attention away from Jeff and his eyes that seemed too kind to belong to a player. He'd be a nice Halloween treat for some other lucky lady. Like the woman next to him, checking him out while her hubby supervised the pumpkin painting.

But the feeling of regret was still there by the end of the day. Jerry approached me as I was leaving. "Can you whip up some more arrangements? They're selling well. Maybe do something with the pumpkins, too? Grab whatever you need before you leave. We've got a bumper crop this year."

"Great." And that was another reason not to go out to dinner. I was too busy with my crafty creations. *Right.* But the news that my work was selling was reason to smile. And it inspired me to make them even better.

I stopped by Your Heart's Desire florist on my way home. So far, I'd been using silk flowers in my arrangements. I wanted to see how fresh flowers would do, and an empty pumpkin would be the perfect "container," so I brought a pumpkin in with me to match up with flowers.

Browsing through the bouquets on display, I decided to get some cattails, mums, gerbera daisies, and purple asters. I smiled at the woman behind the counter. "Excuse me, I'm looking to make some arrangements with pumpkins. Can I buy bulk flowers from you?"

She set down her floral shears. "I usually don't sell from my stock, but if you bring me a few arrangements to sell, I'll make an exception and give you a discount."

"Sounds great. I'm Marnie James."

She offered her hand. "Lynn Preston. How does twenty dollars per arrangement sound?"

"Great." The pumpkins were free, and I'd limit myself to eight dollars worth of flowers per pumpkin, along with some wild Queen Anne's Lace growing along the road in front of my house. *See? I don't need a man. I'm plenty busy with other things.*

***

The flowers were a nice distraction, but I mentally kicked myself later that night as I ate my frozen dinner-for-one. What would've been the harm in going out with a nice, funny guy? A guy who was also divorced and knew how hard it was being out there alone, trying to find love again?

Only, I *wasn't* trying. Lots of women never remarried. Like my best friend's mother divorced at twenty-six and never remarried. She'd never even had another boyfriend as far as we knew. Maybe I'd be one of those women. *Not with Jeff. Don't waste your time.* I sighed, and tossed the remains of the not-so-satisfying lasagna in the trash.

I cleared off the kitchen table and spread out my flowers and pumpkins. I'd brought home a dozen, and I'd spent seventy-five dollars on flowers. I winced, thinking of that credit card statement. Hopefully, shoppers would like fresh flowers, too. Then I panicked. Maybe they only liked the silks because they could use them year after year?

I've got to make these really unique. After scooping out the insides and cutting off the tops, the pumpkins looked rather boring in comparison to the pretty vases and baskets I'd been using with the silk flowers.

Admiring the scalloped edge of a vase we'd gotten for our wedding—and wondering if I should get rid of it—I copied the pattern on the pumpkin. On another, I etched in blacks cats, stars, and moons. I inserted absorbent oasis material in the bottom of the pumpkin to hold the water, and arranged the flowers.

The night flew by. As I stepped back to admire my work, I realized it was midnight. I collapsed in bed, exhausted. But I had time enough to think about what an evening with Jeff would have been like, instead. Strange; in the ten months since my divorce, I hadn't lain in bed thinking about anyone.

***

I dropped off four arrangements at the floral shop

the next morning. Lynn was thrilled. "Can you make more? These are gorgeous. I'm increasing your payment to twenty-five dollars each." She set one in her display window at the front of the store.

At Gruber's, the eight arrangements sold out before the day was over and Jerry insisted I take three-dozen pumpkins home and restock some the next day. My spirits were high when I drove to Bill's to pick up Chelsea. Then I saw them playing catch in the front yard—with the new girlfriend.

Good feelings gone. I took a deep breath, got out of the car, and faked a smile.

Chelsea ran over. "Mommy! I caught the ball seven times!"

"She's a natural," said the too-pretty brunette tossing a ball in the air.

I sucked in a breath and walked over to them. "Hi, I'm Chelsea's mother, Marnie."

"I'm Pam. Nice to meet you." Shaking her hand, I noticed her slim fingers were perfectly manicured. Bill always gave me a hard time when I'd spent money on a manicure.

Bill wrapped his arm around her waist. "We had a great time."

My throat tightened, watching him so happy with someone. Had he ever looked like that with me? "Good, I'm glad."

Bill kissed Pam on the cheek. "She's a natural with kids."

I felt my eyes widen and my stomach tumble. "Super." I looked at Chelsea. "We should get going, sweetie."

"Aww. I'm having fun with Pam."

Oh, child. Just kick me in the stomach. It'd hurt less.

Bill turned to me. "Hey, I know next week it's your weekend with Chelsea, but Pam is the PR director for the hockey team and has tickets to the game Saturday. It's family night. Can we swap weeks? I can pick her up and bring her back."

Chelsea looked at me and stuck out her bottom lip. "Please, Mommy?"

I was outnumbered. I didn't want to seem like an insecure spoilsport. "Sure."

"Yay!"

Pam wrinkled her cute nose. "Thanks so much, it's really kind of you."

"No problem." Oh, I wanted to find something wrong with this woman. But she was beautiful, considerate, and nice to my kid. And Bill seemed wild about her. I wouldn't have been surprised if he called me later that night to thank me for breaking up our marriage.

***

Chelsea and I usually had a special dinner the night after she came back from her dad's, but I was so busy with my flower order that we just had pizza. She helped me scoop out the seeds and chattered on the whole time about how cool and fun and pretty Pam was.

The knot in my stomach grew tighter and tighter. Bill was moving on with his life and I was getting cozy with flowers? I'd spent my Saturday night covered in pumpkin seeds. I felt like Cinderella, alright—Cinderella before the fairy-godmother-makeover. And I didn't think she'd be showing up anytime soon. I thought about Jeff's business card in my purse. I wouldn't have to find a sitter for Chelsea since she'd be with her dad. I could go to the party with Jeff.

I promised myself I'd call him the next day.

***

I started dialing his number and hung up—three times. I hadn't called a guy since Jimmy Nelson, back in high school. Bill and I were in college when we met at the concert, and married right after. My dating experience was weak. But I sucked up my courage and let the phone ring without hanging up.

My chest was tight when he answered and I cleared my throat. "Hi Jeff, it's Marnie. From the party? And the pumpkin patch?" *Man, I'm a dork.*

"Hey, Marnie. What are you wearing?"

"Excuse me?" Was this the right Jeff?

"I'm assuming you've got a costume on. You usually do."

I laughed, relieved it was another one of his goofy jokes. "It's just me today. But, I do have a costume in mind for the party this weekend. Is the invitation still open?"

"Yes, of course."

"Great. It'll be fun."

"I'll pick you up at six."

I gave him directions to my place and downed a glass of wine.

***

It was a long week, waiting for the party. My arrangements sold out at the florist and I had to restock them at Gruber's, too, for the weekend rush. I didn't want to go to the party as a dumpy cat, or a pumpkin. I needed something sexy and cute. With my flower earrings, I bought a revealing pirate costume.

But as I got dressed Saturday night, my confidence was floundering. My cleavage was spilling out of the laced-up bodice. Did I look sexy or chubby? I wasn't sure. The red and white striped scarf I'd tied on flattened my hair. I turned around in the mirror several times, not certain if I looked hot or not. I hadn't dressed to impress in years.

Jeff showed up at my door dressed as a cowboy, holding a gift box. "Evening ma'am." He tipped his hat. "Since vampires don't do it for you, I thought I'd try something different."

I led him inside. "What happened to the Smarties?"

"Trey ate them all."

"Damn kids."

"You look great." His gaze took me in from head to toe. "I can't promise I won't make any plundering jokes. Or booty jokes. That'd be too hard." Then he

20

remembered he was holding a box. "A little something for you. I was going to get roses, but that's predictable. And you're anything but predictable." His eyes twinkled. "This made me think of you and your love of pumpkins."

I took the box from him and opened it. I laughed. "Oh, my God." It was one of my pumpkin arrangements. "This is incredible."

"I know, I thought so, too. It's like a little work of art."

"I mean, I made this. I sell them at the orchard and at Your Heart's Desire."

His smile fell. "I bought you something you made?" He scrunched his eyebrows together. "Does that even count, now?"

"Of course! Come here." I led him into the kitchen where my handiwork was still spread out. "It's something new I've been trying."

He picked up a pumpkin I'd started etching. "Nice work. You're really talented."

"Thanks." He was just piling up the points. Despite the campy Halloween costume, he looked handsome in his cowboy hat, and those chaps accented nice thigh muscles. I cleared my throat. "Should we get going?"

He held out his arm and tipped his hat. "Don't mind if we do."

The party was fun, and Jeff had everyone laughing, pretending to hold up the place when we'd first arrived and demanding drinks. He introduced me to all his friends, and I heard plenty of funny stories from his high school days. It wasn't surprising to learn he'd been voted class clown.

"Seriously, I didn't think tater tots would stick to the ceiling!" he said. "Those were really hard to clean off and the janitor didn't even help me."

When he excused himself to use the bathroom, a blonde dressed as a mermaid sauntered over to me. Now *she* knew how to pull off sexy. She held out her hand.

21

"Hi, I'm Vicky Givens. I knew Jeff back in high school."
She shrugged. "We dated, actually. How long have you
two been together?"

She was sending off some major territorial vibes. My
throat tightened. "This is our first date."

"Oh. Good luck. Even back in high school he was a
heartbreaker. Not surprising that he's been married
twice." She adjusted the tail of her costume.

"Twice?" I hoped my eyes weren't bulging.

"You didn't know?" She bit her lip. "Oops. Sorry."
She shrugged. "Maybe you'll be lucky number three."
She excused herself and sauntered over to a group in the
corner.

My heart was in my stomach. Of course he didn't
want to get married again. He had *two* failed marriages. I
swallowed hard. Could I ever have faith in a relationship
with a twice-divorced guy? A guy who'd already told me
didn't want to get married again? He was exactly the kind
of guy I should be avoiding.

Of course, when he walked back in the room, my
heart ignored all that nonsense flying around my head.
Just enjoy the night. Maybe he'd be a rebound guy; a good
guy to help me find my dating-legs again. I felt like I had
a little devil on one shoulder and an angel on the other
arguing over what I should do.

The party wound down after midnight, and Jeff
drove me home. I looked up at the full moon lighting up
the sky. It would be very easy to fall under its romantic
spell. I snuck a glance at Jeff. *Yeah, very easy.*

My heart sped up as we got closer to my house. Was
a good night kiss par-for-the-course these days? Would
he be expecting more? I took a deep breath. That was
another reason to stay single; I hadn't gotten an updated
version of the dating rules. Would I now be required to
get a Brazilian wax every month? I wrinkled my nose at
that thought. Then I remembered the blah, beige bra I
was wearing. Certainly, my underwear wasn't cute
enough to be back on the dating scene. No, I wasn't

prepared for this. It'd been a mistake.

But when he pulled in my driveway, I surprised myself by saying, "Do you want to come in?"

Who was in charge here? My hormones, clearly—or the devil on my shoulder.

Jeff turned in his seat to face me. "I'd love to, but I'm going to take it slow with you. I know you're nervous about dating again. So, as much as I'd like to live up to my plundering jokes, I'm going to kiss you goodnight and hopefully see you again next weekend."

His directness took my breath away. He leaned over the console in the front seat, took my face in his hands and kissed me. It wasn't just a goodnight peck. It was a long, demanding kiss that left my lips tingling and my insides tightly coiled.

"Wow," I said, when our lips parted. "Are you sure you don't want to come in?" My voice sounded smoky.

He slid off my pirate cap and ran his fingers through my hair. "I definitely want to come in. But good things are worth waiting for. I'll call you this week." He got out of the car, and opened the door for me.

Walking me to my front porch, I was surprised how giddy I felt. And to think I wasn't going to go out with him? He kissed me again, this time just a brush of his lips against mine. "Goodnight, Jeff."

"Goodnight my sweet wench."

I nudged him with my elbow. "I'm not that kind of pirate." *But I might be, if you'd just come inside....* But he walked back to his car and I let myself inside.

I slumped on the couch and sighed. I'd survived my first post-divorce date.

But the next morning I felt like Cinderella, again. The magic was gone as I remembered the mermaid's tale: Jeff had been married twice.

Right, I reminded myself. And not very likely to have a successful third one. There had to be sobering statistics on the success of third marriages floating around on the Internet. If I were ever to tie the knot again, it would have to last. I couldn't go through another heartbreak.

I shoved a flower inside the pumpkin I was working on a little harder than I needed to. The florist and the orchard both placed an even bigger order this week and wanted me to start thinking ahead for Thanksgiving.

It should've been a good distraction from my feelings, but it wasn't. It scared me how attracted I was to him—after one date. *Maybe it's just because you're out of practice. Maybe any date would have seemed great the first time out.* Closing my eyes I remembered that kiss and shook my head. No, this had been different. Maybe things happened faster the second time around?

But this wasn't the second time around. He was only out for fun. He'd told me as much.

***

Yet, I found myself keeping track of the days until he called. When I saw his name on the caller ID Wednesday, I squealed.

"What, Mommy?" Chelsea asked.

"Nothing. I just got a really good idea for a new pumpkin arrangement." *Yeah, that's it. Lie to your daughter.*

"Marnie, I was wondering if you and Chelsea would like to come trick-or-treating with Trey and me this week."

"You just want to see me in another costume, don't you?"

"You're on to me. A lovely clown suit, perhaps?"

"You're sure to lose interest in me once Halloween is over."

"No way." He laughed. "You'll just have to pull out a costume from time to time."

We made arrangements to trick or treat in Jeff's neighborhood, since he had a lot of houses on his street. Now, I was more excited for Halloween than Chelsea. Before the big day, I brought another order of pumpkins into the florist.

"Those look great! They sell out almost as soon as

24

you bring them in," Lynn said.

"You'll never believe it, but this guy I went out with brought me one of my arrangements on our first date. Isn't that hilarious?"

She snapped her fingers. "Oh yeah, I remember. Was it Jeff Williams?"

I nodded, surprised she knew.

"He's in here a lot."

Her phone rang and she answered it as my stomach fell. *He's in here a lot?* What was that supposed to mean? I wanted to press her for more details, but it was clear she was going to be on the phone for a while.

I left the shop with a heavy heart. My hot, funny, guy was a twice-divorced, flower-shop-regular—who never wanted to get married again. *What are you doing?*

I'd promised we'd go trick-or-treating, so there was no getting out of that. Chelsea was looking forward to it. But that would be our last date. I was setting myself up for heartbreak—and there was no guarantee I'd bounce back when it ended. I felt like an old pair of control pantyhose with only so much holding power left.

* * *

Trick-or-treating was fun, despite my worries. Jeff had dressed up like a mummy and let the kids unwrap him as we walked from house to house.

He opened a Hershey's kiss and brought it to my mouth. Tentatively, I sunk my teeth into it. He leaned toward me and whispered, "You're the most beautiful gypsy I've ever seen, but I really liked that pirate costume."

I whispered back. "Chelsea hasn't seen that much of my cleavage since she was breast feeding, and I didn't want to shock your son. You're probably not ready for the birds-and-the-bees talk yet."

He laughed. "It's been a while. I don't think I remember enough to tell him."

I gave him a funny look. Officer Hottie probably had plenty of inappropriate tales to draw from.

We finished make the rounds on his cul-de-sac and stood in front of my car. "Would you guys like to grab a bite to eat?" he asked.

"I've gotta get home. I've got four dozen Thanksgiving arrangements to make tomorrow."

"Need some help? I'm a great pumpkin scooper." He pretended to be spooning out the seeds with big exaggerated motions.

I'd planned on this being our last date. But really, I needed the help. "You sure? My ex used to hate when I was crafty. 'Crappy crafts' he used to call them."

"Another reason to be glad he's your ex. Should I come over after lunch?"

"That would be great."

***

We were elbow-deep in pumpkin guts when I thought about what Lynn had told me. I took a deep breath. "So, I told the gal at the flower shop that you bought me one of my own pumpkins."

He laughed. "It was a surprise for both of us."

I concentrated on cutting the top off the pumpkin. "She says you're in there a lot."

He didn't say anything and Chelsea ran into the kitchen before he could comment.

"Mommy, can we have popcorn?" she asked, hopping from foot to foot.

"Sure, honey." And the moment was gone. I didn't want to sound like a nag bringing it up again. But he hadn't denied it, and he hadn't given me a reason why he was there so often.

Jeff showed the kids how to make popcorn balls with corn syrup and butter. Before I knew it, dinnertime rolled around and we went out for Chinese. When we got home at nine, he snuck in a quick kiss.

"Can I see you next weekend?"

I wanted to—but I also didn't. I'd end it next weekend. "Sure."

But I didn't get the chance; he called in the middle of

the week and left a voicemail, canceling our date. "I'm not going to be able to make it. I'm really sorry. It's just … it's a bad time. Hopefully, we can get together soon."

It's for the best. Maybe he was getting spooked, too.

When he called again, I let it go to voicemail. "Want to try to get together this Saturday?" he asked.

Later, I called back and left a message. "I can't, I've got Chelsea this weekend and I'm really busy with my arrangements." Hopefully, things would just taper off with him. But I doubted if I'd find another guy who'd interest me as much as Jeff.

I pulled into the floral shop the week before Thanksgiving and almost hit another car. Jeff was walking out with a bunch of flowers. Not roses, but a nice mixed arrangement. I wondered if he'd been seeing someone else all along.

Not that it mattered. We hadn't gotten beyond a quick kiss. It had never been anything serious. Still, my heart deflated. I drove home. Lynn would have to wait a few hours for her arrangements, because watching your crush buy flowers for someone else is a definite way to squash your feelings.

When I brought the arrangements back a while later, Lynn brushed off her hands. "Do you have a minute to talk?"

Oh, no. She wasn't going to mention that Jeff had bought flowers for someone else, was she? Too embarrassing. "What's up?"

"I need help."

"Sounds serious."

She laughed. "I mean, in the shop. I need to hire someone to put together arrangements, and I'm expanding our gift section. I'll match what you're making at the hotel as long as you bring that creativity of yours here and whip up some more incredible stuff."

I leaned against the counter. "Are you serious?"

She nodded. "I'm hoping you could start in a few weeks, before the Christmas rush."

"What about health insurance?"

"I get mine through the Chamber of Commerce. I can pick up a plan for you."

Practical, safe-playing me was thinking, no, no of course not. But the part of me I'd hidden away for years pushed past the doubt and worry and said, "Yes, I'll take it. I'll put in my two weeks' notice tomorrow." I slapped my hand over my mouth.

"Are you sure?"

Even while I was muzzling myself, I managed to nod yes.

She shrieked and clapped. "I'm so excited! This is going to be wonderful. I'll put you down on the schedule for two weeks from tomorrow. The day before Thanksgiving. Is that okay?"

Again, I could only nod yes.

I drove home, trying to remember the last time my heart felt so light and hopeful. It almost felt like falling in love—as far as I could remember. Maybe that's the best I could hope for—loving what I did for a living. Forget the men.

My manager wasn't happy about losing me at the office, but he admitted, "It's probably a good move. I've never seen you this excited, I'm happy for you."

The day before Thanksgiving was a busy day for my first day. We sold all but two of my pumpkins, and I made some new cornucopia arrangements with fruits and flowers.

I went home feeling better than I had in years. Jeff called again, and this time, I answered.

"Hey, stranger. How are you? Not dressed as a Turkey, are you?"

I flopped on the couch. "No, exhausted from my new job. Lynn hired me at her floral shop."

"That's great. I go there whenever I need flowers or beautiful pumpkin arrangements."

My smile disappeared, remembering him walking out with a bouquet of flowers. But I pushed the bad feeling away. Jeff and I hadn't been a couple. For all I knew, he was just being nice to me, helping me ease back into the dating game. "I'm really excited about it."

"I don't know what you've got planned tomorrow for the holiday, but Trey is with his mom, and the rest of my family's out of town. I usually make the trip, but not this year. If you're in the same boat, why don't you stop by tomorrow for Thanksgiving?"

"I'm going to my Aunt's house. But thanks."

"No problem." He paused for a moment. "I get the sense it's not working between us. Am I right?"

I opened my mouth then closed it. "I'm just not ready." I'd been right. It was too hard to be out there.

He must've known what I was thinking. "Don't wait too long, Marnie. You're going to miss a lot of good times if you give in to your fear."

"Thanks, Jeff. For everything." After hanging up, my good, new-job feelings were overshadowed by the disappointment that I wouldn't see him again.

***

I brought one of my arrangements to Thanksgiving dinner, and my relatives ooh'd and aah'd and were supportive of my job change.

"If only you could meet a nice man," Aunt Ruthie said, patting my hand with as much concern as if I'd just announced some sort of terminal diagnosis.

I forced a smile. "Too busy for a man. And I'm happy, really." God, did that sound like a lie.

"Did you hear Ginny is moving to Florida with her boyfriend?" she asked.

I looked over at my cousin, Ginny, sitting on the floor next to her boyfriend. My little cousin was moving? She was five years younger than me. Could she really be old enough to move south with a guy? I tallied up her age in my head; yep, she was twenty-three.

She looked at me and smiled with a little, *Crazy, right?* shrug.

"What are you going to do down there?" I asked.

"Another bakery?" She turned up her hands. "I'll figure it out when I get there. I just didn't want to be apart from Ryan, and when he got his job down there, we knew we didn't want to do the long-distance thing." She took a shaky breath and smiled.

Her boyfriend stood up. "I'm getting a refill. Want one, honey?"

"Another eggnog would be great, thanks."

He walked away and I scurried over to sit next to her. "You've never even had your own place! And you're moving across the country? How long have you been dating?"

Her smile slipped for a moment. "Ten months. But isn't love always about taking chances?"

The words hit my heart. She was right. And I'd never find it again if I wasn't willing to take a chance.

But could I take a chance on Jeff? I nibbled my lip. I'd taken a chance changing jobs, and look how that had made me feel—re-energized, excited, alive. Just thinking about Jeff made me swoon. I had to talk to him. He was worth a try even if I might get hurt in the process.

I stood up. "I've got to go."

Ginny gave me a look. "We haven't even had dessert. Where are you going?"

"Taking a chance." I said my goodbyes and bundled up a few pieces of pie to share with Jeff.

Driving over to his house, I decided to be upfront and ask all the questions that had been bothering me. I just wished I could slow down my heart. Was I more thrilled or scared? I couldn't tell.

When I pulled into his driveway, my insides were twisting and my breath quickened, but I had nothing to lose.

I rang the doorbell and was delighted to see Jeff's face morph from surprise to pleasure when he answered. "What are you doing here?"

I looked up at him; my words came out in a whisper. "Taking a chance."

Grinning, he looked me up and down. "Damn. No pilgrim costume?"

"Careful, or I won't share this." I handed him the plate of desserts.

He stepped back to let me in. "Now you're speaking my language." He led me into the family room, where the football game was playing. He set down the plate and gestured for me to sit on the couch.

I had so many questions for him. *Might as well get to it.* I'd wasted enough time already. I gripped the arm of the couch. "Are you seeing anyone?"

He crossed his arms. "I thought I was seeing you, but that didn't seem to work out. I'm so glad you're here, though. I thought we really clicked."

"Me too. That's why I was surprised to see you leave the florist with a bunch of flowers. Plus, Lynn said you're in there a lot. So, I figured you must be seeing someone who's getting flowers instead of pumpkins." My voice came out soft and squeaky, betraying the calm I was faking.

He took a deep breath and looked down. He didn't say anything for a few moments. "They're for my first wife."

My chest tightened. Was he still involved with her? "Vicky at the party said you've been divorced twice. Why didn't you tell me?"

Leaning forward, he splayed his hands on the coffee table. "I've been married twice. But my first wife died."

I sucked in a breath, replaying her words. "That's right. She said you'd been married twice. I just assumed…." I reached for his arm, setting my hand on his soft, flannel shirt. "I'm so sorry. What happened?"

His gaze shifted to the back window, staring out into the dark night. "We were coming home from a party. I fell asleep at the wheel. Walked away without a scratch. But she'd forgotten to put on her seatbelt." He closed his eyes and his face twisted in pain. "It happened right after Halloween. That's why I cancelled our plans that

31

weekend. It was too close to the anniversary of her death."

I touched his arm. "I'm so sorry, Jeff."

He nodded. "I leave flowers at her grave for her birthday. Our anniversary. I just want her to know I'm sorry." He looked at me. "That's why I'm buying flowers so often." He shook his head. "And that's why my second marriage broke up. And it's the reason I haven't wanted to get married again. I just can't forget about Kelly. I didn't stop loving her when she died."

"Of course not. And you don't have to forget about her."

He looked up at the ceiling. I wondered if he was fighting back tears. He sighed. "It just seems to get in the way of other relationships."

I scooted closer to him. "You just haven't found the right relationship."

He shrugged. "After my divorce, I thought, I can't do this again. So I try to make everything fun and jokes so it can't get serious, you know?"

I nodded and smiled. "And I'm too afraid to have any fun at all." The things he'd said to me over the past few weeks made sense now. "But I remember some good advice you gave me and clumsy equestrians everywhere. And here I am. You're right. We can just have fun."

He reached for my hand. "Since I met you, I've been thinking having fun isn't enough anymore. I want more than that. But I'm nervous." He laughed softly. "Can't believe I admitted that."

I laughed. "I'm sure we can find a solution in the middle."

He took my hand in his. "Good. It's worth a try."

I squeezed his hand, a shiver shooting through me. "It's scary, isn't it?"

Nodding, he blew out a long breath. "But it was even scarier to think I'd never be able to do this again."

He tipped my chin up and brushed his lips across mine. Then he trailed his kisses over to my ear. "You don't have your pirate costume in the car, do you?"

I giggled, chasing away the fear, realizing what I was truly afraid of—putting my heart out there and never feeling like this again. "I'll bring it next time," I whispered.

Next time. It felt good saying that.

"Should I go put on my cop uniform?"

I laughed. "No, this is good for now." I patted his arm. "Perfect, actually."

"Good. Because I'm pulling a twelve-hour shift tomorrow. It's Black Friday." He rolled his eyes. "Nightmare. But I'm going to be thankful for this right now."

His lips crushed against mine, and I held on to him as we started this crazy, scary wonderful ride, hopeful where it would take us.

"Holiday Rush"
By Lisa Scott

Lindy Richards pulled into the Save Land parking lot and let out a tremendous sigh. Christmas music was playing on the radio already, but she certainly wasn't in the holiday spirit—not after the Black Friday from hell. She turned off the car and reached for her purse. It was wedged between the console and her seat. When tugging didn't free it, she pawed through the contents, pulling out lipsticks and receipts, gum and tissues, and finally managed to fish out her credit card. That's all she needed for the world's fastest shopping blitz, anyway.

It was ten minutes to nine, and somehow, the day just kept getting worse. Scheduling her first blind date after the busiest shopping day in the world was her first mistake; wearing cheap tights from the clearance bin was the second. But Lindy wasn't one to pass up an end-of-the-season sale. She'd been raised a bargain shopper, and it was a hard habit to break even though her wardrobe these days could be featured on the pages of Vogue. Or at least Elle.

The upscale boutique Lindy managed wasn't top on most Black Friday shoppers' lists—her clientele didn't wait for sales—but Sublime had been busy that day, and she hadn't been adequately staffed to handle the crowds. Which was why she was late to meet Spencer in person for the first time. Drinks and maybe dessert? She wiggled in her seat just thinking of him, with the dreamy profile picture, a love of New Zealand wines and a fondness for foreign films. She could learn to like those.

On the ride to the bar, she'd ripped her tights and cut her leg on the broken molding on her car door—the molding she'd been meaning to fix for three months now. The broken strip of trim had left a long gash on her leg, and without realizing is, she'd smeared blood all over the door. *I really need to upgrade my ride.* Just as soon as she stopped buying three-hundred-dollar shoes.

Her roommate Darcy liked to compare her to a shark on a feeding frenzy when she hit the mall. "You need to be reeled in. Seriously," Darcy had told her.

That'll be my New Year's Resolution, Lindy thought. *Maybe.*

She snapped off the broken molding, inspected her leg again, and groaned. Clearly there was no way she could show up with ripped, bloody tights on a first date; third date, *maybe.* But definitely not after Spencer had mentioned his stockpile of bleach wipes. Darcy had raised her eyebrows at that bit of news.

"What?" Lindy had said with a huff. "Opposites attract." *At least he's not going to show up on* Hoarders, she'd thought to herself.

He seemed perfect, and she wasn't going to blow this because of a wardrobe malfunction and a flesh wound. Why didn't these kinds of things happen to anyone else? She frowned at the blood on the door, and the bloody fingerprints she was now leaving on the steering wheel.

With ten minutes to spare before Save Land Department store closed, she'd rush inside to grab a new pair of tights. She thought about wearing sunglasses— just in case anyone spotted her there. The manager of the chicest boutique in Rochester shouldn't be cruising a discount department store.

She popped open her glove compartment, dumping out the contents searching for a pair, but came up empty. With credit card in hand, she hopped out, hoping her car would be safe for a few minutes since the driver's door had stopped locking two days earlier. *When it rains it pours—and it's been a tropical storm,* she thought.

A dusting of snow skittered across the parking lot, chilling her toes. She threw out the broken molding, tossed a handful of change from her coat pocket in the Salvation Army kettle, and walked through the sliding doors. Her jaw dropped. The place looked like it'd been looted. She wound her way between wayward shopping carts, empty display racks, and half-stocked supply carts. She grabbed a pack of baby wipes to clean up, and finally found the ladies department, pawing through the meager selection of tights. Her ripped tights were maroon, to go with her forest green wool skirt, but they only had bright red, navy, brown and black to choose from. Figures. She'd have to go with black.

She grabbed a pack in her size and headed for the register, when the cutest leggings caught her eye. Only fifteen dollars? You couldn't buy anything in Sublime for fifteen dollars. Maybe a bottle of designer water. The cheapest piece of clothing they carried was a thirty-dollar pack of socks. Glancing around, she saw that no one was looking and snatched the leggings—in silver, fuchsia, and blue—along with a matching over-sized sweater. She dashed to the dressing room in the far back corner of the store. The attendant must have abandoned her post long ago from the look of things. *Can't blame ya, sister.*

Lindy bustled into the dressing room and thought about calling Spencer to tell him she'd be late. That's when she remembered she'd left her purse in the car—with her cell. Oh well, she'd be fashionably late in her unfashionable tights.

She slipped on the leggings, trying different combinations with the sweaters and decided blue and silver looked best, but she'd never ever admit where she'd gotten them. She shuddered, imagining what her boss, Michaela, would say if she found out Lindy was wearing an outfit from Save-Freaking-Land.

She turned around in the mirror examining the perfect fit. Cute was cute, no matter the cost, right? Of course, that hadn't been her opinion when she was a kid and her father could only afford to clothe her in garage sale finds and hand-me downs. The memory hit her like a brick. She'd never forget queen bee Vicky Givens teasing mercilessly about her the three-seasons-old coat.

She dropped onto the bench seat in the dressing room and stared at the worn blue industrial carpet.

Hangers littered the floor. She took a deep breath, waiting for the bad feelings to slink away. After Lindy had learned how to sew in home economics class, she'd shortened ugly skirts, and jazzed up plain shirts with trim. Several girls started doing the same thing—even a few who could afford the latest Abercrombie and Hollister wardrobes. But still, she'd always regretted not being able to wear the latest fashions like Vicky Givens and Tiffany Carter. Once, Tiffany wore a two hundred dollar skirt just one time, before deciding the color was 'pukey.'

Shaking away the memory, she blinked, felt better, and decided this was the best chance to change into her tights. She'd pay for them on the way out. She tore open the package, when the lights in the dressing room dimmed.

She swore to herself, trying to get the tights on quicker. Hopping on one foot to pull them up, she heard the fabric rip and swore again. *Fine. I'll wear the sweater and leggings.* She quickly changed into the outfit, scooped up her own clothes, and dashed for the changing room door to head out and pay for it all.

She tried to turn the handle. This time she swore aloud; the changing room door was locked. She pounded on the door. "Hello! Someone's still in here! Hello?" She checked her watch. It was nine-fifteen. She probably had fifteen more minutes before they closed the store.

But shaking the handle and hollering didn't get anyone's attention. They were surely all up front, closing down the registers, ready to go home and soak their feet. No one was back here. Once again, she reached for the purse she wasn't holding and the phone that was in it— currently, both stuck between the seats, with her keys—in her unlocked car.

Stupid, stupid, stupid. She tried tripping the lock on the door with her credit card, like she'd seen a few detectives do on TV. Then she tried the straightened end of a hanger, but still no luck. She was stuck inside the Save Land changing room when she should be enjoying a drink with the cute, cultured, hygienic guy she'd finally agreed to meet.

Black Friday had been a very bad day indeed. She curled up on the seat in the biggest changing room and finally let the tears loose.

Then the lights went out.

***

The phone woke Alex at six-fifteen in the morning. He groaned. He wasn't due back at the store until noon. *This better be good—or really, really bad.* He fumbled for his cell on the nightstand. "Hello?"

"Hey boss, it's Laurel. Sorry to bother you, but I thought you should know the news is reporting live across the street from our parking lot. Some woman is missing, and her car is in our lot, covered in blood."

Shit. "Thanks. I'll be right there." He fished out a fresh suit from the closet and cursed his father once more for sending him here to earn his wings. He belonged in New York or Philly, or even Boston for crying out loud. But Rochester? With missing shoppers as breaking news?

Alex arrived just in time to hear the tail end of the 6:30 live report. "Ms. Richards, manager of the Sublime boutique downtown, left work and was expected on a blind date last night, where she failed to show up. Her roommate reported her missing last night. When detectives found this abandoned, they linked it to her. The car was ransacked, blood covered the door and steering wheel, and her keys and cell phone were inside. We'll keep you updated on the very latest."

It was more serious than he thought. He hoped the woman was okay. The photographer flicked off his light. Alex dodged the reporter and headed for the cop in charge of the scene. "I'm Alexander Whitney, the manager here."

The policeman shook his hand. "Detective Jeff Williams. We've been trying to contact someone from the store. We want to take a look at your security tapes. You've got one on the parking lot, right?"

"We do. Let me show you." He unlocked the store, hoping to God that Save Land had nothing to do with this. His father would probably keep him here even longer, blaming him for the bad publicity, as if Alex had snatched the woman himself.

After flicking on the store lights, he led the detective to the security office in the back of the store. Had someone really been abducted in their parking lot? The thought made him sick. He opened the office, wondering if anything helpful was on the tape. But with blood in her car, it didn't look good. "Do they suspect the blind date?" he asked the cop.

"We interviewed him, but he has a solid alibi. He was at the bar waiting for her."

Alex nodded and turned on the lights in the office. Then he paused, cocking his head. "Did you hear that?"

The detective's hand flew to his gun and the two of them ran to the changing rooms. Someone was inside, pounding on the door. He heard a woman cry, "Help me! I'm stuck inside here!"

Alex fumbled with the keys and unlocked the door. A tall woman tumbled out and fell into his arms. Instinctively, he wrapped his arms around her and they stared at each other for a moment. Her dark hair was tousled and he fought the urge to brush it off her cheek.

"I'm Alex Whitney, the manager here. Are you okay?"

She narrowed her eyes then balled up her fists. "No, I am not okay! Some nitwit locked me in the changing room last night! What kind of operation are you running here?" She pulled herself out of Alex's embrace, tugging her sweater back into place.

He felt the blood drain from his face. *He* had locked the changing rooms last night—without making sure they were empty; without following store procedure.

No time for regret. He smoothed his tie back in place after the impromptu pummeling. His management training had him thinking damage control. Save Land could be held liable. He'd be held liable—by his father, if not this woman. He had to think fast.

The cop interrupted his frazzled train of thought. "I assume you're Lindy Richards?" he asked.

She tipped up her chin. "I am."

Alex ran a trembling hand through his hair. "Are you okay, Miss Richards?" he finally managed to ask. "What happened?" He got caught in her big blue eyes and disheveled hair. Even with the bloodshot eyes, she was pretty.

Her shoulders slumped and she groaned, a bit of the anger seeping off her. "I stopped in right before the store closed to get some tights and I tried on some clothes—"

"—The clothes you're wearing," Alex said, gesturing to her outfit.

She put her hands on her hips. "Yes. And next thing I know, someone locked the door. I yelled, but no one heard me."

The cop crossed his arms. "What about the blood in the car? Your purse and cell phone were inside. It looked like an abduction."

She sighed, looking up at the ceiling. "I cut my leg, ripped my stockings and that's why I had to dash in here."

"On the way to your blind date?" Alex said.

She stepped back. "How do you know that?"

"It was on the news."

Her eyes widened and she turned three shades paler. "What was on the news?"

"You, missing," Alex said.

Her hand flew to her mouth and she shook her head. "I really need to use the restroom."

"Follow me." Alex led her to the front of the store. He held the door open for her and smiled. "I'll make sure you don't get locked in."

Her eyes narrowed. She didn't look half bad for spending the night in a dressing room. Hell, she looked beautiful—and pissed off. Not exactly the best profile

40

for the woman holding his future in her hands.

Once she disappeared behind the door, the cop looked around nervously. "Say, you don't sell Mrs. Santa costumes here, do you?"

Was Alex the only one who wasn't nuts for the holidays? He gave the officer the once over. "*Mrs. Clause?*"

The cop shook his head. "Not for me. It's for a friend. She likes to dress up." He cleared his throat. "So, how'd Lindy end up locked inside?"

Alex frowned. "Someone forgot to check that the dressing rooms were clear before locking the door."

The cop whistled. "I'd hate to be that person."

"Yeah. Me, too."

***

Lindy squeezed into the nearest stall. A half-hour longer in that dressing room, and things would have been messy. She wrinkled her nose. At least it was over, and the nausea had subsided, so she wasn't going to puke. But she was embarrassed, angry, and stiff from her restless night trying to sleep propped up against the wall—and trying to pretend germs weren't coating the wall. That was one of the bad things about working in retail—she knew what people did in dressing rooms.

She splashed water on her face and fluffed her hair. Not because the manager was handsome. What a jerk, wearing Gucci when he was managing a Save Land. Or mis-managing was more like it. Who did he think he was, selling discount clothes and wearing a two-thousand-dollar suit? He looked fantastic in it, but still, rather uppity of him.

Desperate to go home and shower before heading back to the boutique, she hurried out of the bathroom and realized she was still wearing the sweater and leggings, price tags and all. Too tired to care, she headed for the exit.

Alex's gaze went from head to toe. *After all that, he's worried I'm leaving without paying!* She tipped her nose in the air. "I'm not stealing them. I was detained on my way to the register last night. I certainly don't want them anymore, but I've worn them, so I'll buy them." She held out her credit card. "Let's go ring it up."

He held up a hand like a traffic cop. "No need. Keep them, compliments of Save Land." It was bad timing but he couldn't help but grin

She rolled her eyes. "Makes it all worthwhile."

"Let's get outside and call off the search for you," the detective said.

She clutched her bundle of clothes and her coat as they headed outside. Alex held it up so she could slip her arms in the gorgeous red Burberry.

Three news crews ran toward the building, leaving footprints in the freshly fallen snow toward the building, their microphones leading the way. "Is that the missing woman?" one of them called out.

"Is she okay?" another asked.

Lindy's stomach tumbled. She was dreaming. This couldn't be real.

"Turns out our missing woman wasn't abducted," the officer said, hitching up his pants. "She was shopping." He chuckled.

Lindy's eyes were wide and she blinked at the cameras. Then she shook her head, like she might be able to make it all go away. "I needed new tights. I got locked in the changing room." She jerked her thumb over her shoulder.

"You were trying on the tights?" asked a young reporter, wrinkling her nose. "You don't try on *tights*."

Lindy looked away, scratching her head. This was like the time she spent an hour chatting with a hot guy at a wedding only to discover she'd had a sesame seed stuck to her cheek from the hors d'euvres! Excruciatingly embarrassing and hard to believe. "I grabbed a few things at the last minute."

"The new leggings from our Excite! collection. We're letting her keep those, free of charge." Alex smoothed his lapels. "And to apologize for the inconvenience, we'd like to offer you a five-hundred-dollar gift card."

She held up a hand. "That's okay. I don't shop here."

"But, you were last night," said one of the reporters.

"That's right, you're the manager of Sublime," added another, as he scribbled in his notebook, grinning.

"It was an emergency. I was on my way to…" She bit her lip.

"A blind date?" another reporter offered.

She turned to the detective. "Can I go home now?"

"How did she get locked inside? Don't you have procedures to prevent this sort of thing?" one of the reporters asked.

Alex stepped forward. "We do. And I'm afraid with the holiday rush yesterday, those procedures were overlooked. I'll hold an emergency briefing with the staff before we open today. This won't happen again." He grinned so charmingly, Lindy imagined anyone would believe anything this man said.

The reporters finally ran out of questions and hurried back to their news vans to prepare for the next update when Lindy would officially and publicly be named the biggest fool in upstate New York—maybe of all the East coast. She started toward her car, then turned back to face Alex. She was angry, but she really didn't want anyone to get sacked because of her. "Please don't fire whoever did this."

He grinned. "I won't."

She exhaled. "Good."

"Because it was me."

Lindy felt her fists clenching again. She forced a smile, but felt her lips tighten instead. "You. You locked me in." She'd been envisioning some poor old woman beat from a long day who'd skipped closing procedures after the day from black Friday hell—not the smug, sophisticated manager.

43

Pursing his lips, he walked toward her. She gulped and took a step back. He smelled good. She couldn't imagine what *she* smelled like after a night in the stuffy dressing room.

He rubbed his chin. "My apologies. I don't usually close up, but the gal who'd been supervising the dressing rooms nearly collapsed from exhaustion." He shrugged. "I didn't follow our own company procedures. How can I make it up to you? I insist on the gift card."

She marched to her car and flung open the door. "There's no fixing this." She closed her eyes and exhaled. Truthfully, she was at fault, too. She'd left her phone and her purse in the car. She could've called for help if she'd had it. She looked up at him. If he weren't the man responsible for the most humiliating moment of her life, she'd have concocted a few fantasies on the spot; he was hot. "Let's just forget about this." She looked away from his mesmerizing stare, got in her car and drove away, knowing it would be impossible to ever forget this.

She checked her cell on the way home. Spencer had left four messages; the last one from the police station. Lindy cringed. That would be an awkward call to make later. She dialed her sister's number, and she answered on the first ring.

"Hey, I saw you on TV! It's too bad you couldn't have touched up your makeup before you were on camera."

She turned down the road, never more grateful to see her condo complex in the distance. "I'm fine, Jessica, thanks for asking."

"I know you're fine. I saw the TV report."

"Well, I just didn't want you to worry any more."

"I wasn't worried. I didn't know you were missing until I saw the report that you'd been found. I didn't know you shopped at Save Land. I thought you only wore uppity clothes now."

Lindy groaned. "I don't shop there."

"But you were at the store, right?"

"It's been a long night. I'll talk to you later, Jessica." She hung up, wondering what her dad would've said about this if he were still alive. He probably would've found a way to make her laugh about it.

Frowning, she went inside her condo. Darcy was asleep on the couch, her phone in her hand. Lindy felt sick realizing how worried she must have been.

Darcy must have heard her, because she opened her eyes and ran to the door. "You're alive!"

Lindy found herself in a stranglehold. "Where were you?" Darcy demanded.

Lindy sighed. "I got locked in a dressing room." She gulped. "At Save Land." With poor Darcy at her wit's end, she felt even more embarrassed than she had admitting it to the cop and the store manager.

Darcy backed away from her. "Really? When Spencer called here looking for you…" She took a giant gulp of air. "…I thought something horrible had happened. I called the police—I was on the news!" Her cheeks were flush with excitement as she rattled on. "I knew you wouldn't miss your date, so I figured he must have done something to you. And… and… cleaned up the evidence with all those bleach wipes you told me about." She was breathless

Lindy hugged her. "I'm fine."

Darcy sniffed. "So, nothing bad happened at all?" She seemed a bit disappointed.

"No, but something bad will happen if I don't get to work on time." She squinted at the clock on the microwave. It was eight-ten, and she was due at work at nine. She'd have enough time to shower, change—God yes, change—and hopefully, put this whole mess behind her.

"I'm going to bed," Darcy said, clearly disappointed her amateur sleuthing had led to nothing more than an uncomfortable night's sleep for Lindy.

***

She thought she'd be the first one at the boutique,

but she was wrong. The owner, Michaela Marks, was there, dressed to the nines in a couture black Versace suit. *Ooh, sooo pretty, but two sizes too small for me,* Lindy thought. She had no idea it was possible to look that good at nine am. Michaela sat on the couch near the dressing rooms—that did not lock from the outside, thank you very much—and blinked at Lindy when she walked in.

"What are you doing here?" Lindy asked, as breezily as she could. Hard to do when your knees are knocking.

"I'm here to work."

Lindy gulped. Michaela Marks hadn't worked in her own store in three years.

Michaela looked her up and down. "Where's your snazzy outfit I saw this morning?"

Lindy forced a smile and tried to sound breezy. "I know, crazy, right? A girl dashes in for a pair of tights and ends up the lead story on the news." She walked toward the cash register—mostly to grab the counter for support. While Michaela wasn't wearing a coat made of puppies, something about her definitely reeked of Cruella de Ville.

Michaela stood up and glided toward the gorgeous marble counter. "Do you know how foolish my boutique looks right now?" Lindy jerked back as if she'd been struck.

Michaela walked around her and turned on the register. "I'll be running the boutique today. I have to let you go, Lindy." Her French accent sounded more angry than glamorous.

She sucked in a breath. "It was an accident. I'm sorry. People will forget." Lindy hated sounding desperate, but she was. She loved her job, helping people find beautiful clothes, like selecting the perfect dress for a special occasion. It was like being a matchmaker. Sure, some of the women were snotty socialites who didn't deserve such gorgeous outfits. She didn't like that part. And sometimes it seemed obscene to sell someone a suit for two thousand dollars. But still, she loved the clothes.

And the discount! She set her hand on her stomach but it kept flip-flopping.

Michaela slammed the cash register shut. "People will be talking about this for weeks. You've damaged my brand. You're done. No severance pay, and no recommendation."

Lindy backed away toward the door. "I'm sorry."

Michaela didn't even look at her. "You should be."

Lindy bumped open the door with her hip and tumbled outside, blinded by the morning sun; far too bright and cheery for the mess unfolding around her. *How could this be happening?* she wondered. It's the holiday season—the most wonderful time of year. Her favorite season, when magic and miracles happened. Around Christmas, she felt like a little girl again.

Lindy would never forget that incredible year when Santa had brought loads and loads of gifts for her. Things she hadn't even asked for! She figured it was Santa's way of saying sorry her mother had died. At five years old, it was the most logical solution. She'd never had another Christmas like that. But the hope was always there that something like that could happen again.

Clearly, not this year, she mumbled to herself.

"Ah, just the woman I was looking for."

Lindy shaded her eyes and saw Alex Whitney, Save Land manager, heading her way down the sidewalk. She groaned. "Are you coming to lock me in the dressing room *here*?"

"Ah, she's cute and funny. No, that's the first and last time that will happen."

Cute? "If you haven't noticed I'm having a really shitty day. And it's all your fault. Please go away." She shooed him away with her hands.

Somehow, her harsh words didn't seem to affect him. He just kept on smiling which made her even madder. He took another step closer. "I wanted to bring you that gift card. And my apologies. Want to show me your store?"

She folded her arms. "It's not my store anymore. I got fired." She reached for the gift card in his hand. "Turns out, I'll be needing this." That baby went right into her purse.

Alex's smile fell, taking his dimples with it. "You're kidding. She fired you?"

"I embarrassed the boutique beyond repair."

With his hands on his hips, he looked up at the sky sighed. "Let me take you out for coffee. Let's talk about this."

"What's to talk about?"

One side of his mouth curled up. "Maybe I can offer you a spot at our store." Before she could answer, he bustled her into his Lexus.

Her phone rang as his car lurched through the quiet Saturday-morning streets. "Hello?" she answered. *The day couldn't get worse, could it?*

"You're alive. I didn't expect my first blind date to end in a police station."

"Spencer. I'm so sorry. I ripped my stockings and stopped at the store—"

He interrupted her. "I know. I saw the news."

"Oh." How many people watched the Saturday morning news, anyway? "So, do you want to try again next week?" She chewed her thumbnail; a habit she'd kicked a decade ago. She sat on her hand.

He was quiet for a moment. "Remember how you talked about signs the other day?"

Lindy had told Spencer she thought it was a sign they should go out because she'd had a record-breaking sales day the same day he'd responded to her online profile. He'd told her it was sweet, and agreed. "I remember," she said.

"This is a sign things are not meant to be. I'm glad you're okay, but this isn't going to work out. Especially after seeing the inside of your car on TV."

God, they showed that? Tears pricked her eyes and she blinked them away. "I understand. Goodbye, Spencer."

She hung up and dropped her head back against the seat. She looked at Alex. "And I thought the worst was over when you showed up this morning."

"Who was that?"

"The blind date I stood up. We've been talking online for three months. I really liked him. Now he doesn't want to meet me." She glared at him and poked her finger against an impressively hard bicep. "You cost me my guy and the gorgeous Hermes scarf I was saving up for at Sublime. I had it set aside and everything." She crossed her arms. "I'm not sure which is worse."

He totally ignored her pouting. "Wouldn't have figured you for the online dating type."

"What's that supposed to mean?"

***

Alex weighed his words carefully. "You're sophisticated and beautiful. You'd be the last person I'd expect to find online." *Trust me, I'd be online if I'd known.*

She drew in a sharp breath. "Well, now I'm unemployed. I'll have tons of people lining up to go out with me."

He pulled into the parking lot of Bean Happy and looked at her. "We'd love to have you on board." He was desperate, really, to hire her. It seemed like the only solution to keep this from becoming a PR nightmare; and to keep his father from permanently assigning him to this post.

She closed her eyes. "I am *not* working for Save Land. I shouldn't even have been shopping there."

He drummed the steering wheel. "What do you have against my store, anyway? You seemed pretty happy with the fifteen-dollar leggings."

"It was an exceptional find in the midst of a mediocre buffet of off-the-rack clothes. It shocked me as much as it shocked you."

"Really, don't hold back." But he couldn't help grinning. He hopped out and opened the door for her, and was greeted by the sight of her long, slim legs. He sucked in a breath.

They walked into the coffee shop and sat at one of the bistro tables. "What can I get you?"

Lindy rubbed her temples. "Does anything here come with alcohol?"

He laughed. "I don't think so, but I'm sure there's a market for it."

"I'll take a chai latte."

He got their drinks, and sat down across from her, smiling again.

"Do you think this whole thing is funny?"

He tried to suppress his grin, but couldn't. "I don't. I just find you—interesting."

She rolled her eyes. "No need to schmooze. I'm not going to sue. I'm not that kind of girl."

"I'm sorry. Really. But you are in a jam." He decided to hedge his bet. "We've been looking to expand the management team at this location. Why don't I show you the ropes and train you as assistant manager?"

She opened her mouth, but he didn't give her a chance to protest. "The salary starts at forty-five thousand with stock options, and given last night's incident, I'm sure I can entice corporate to include a ten-thousand dollar signing bonus."

Her frown disappeared and she fluttered her fingertips on the table. "Save Land is open three hundred sixty five days a year, isn't it? You're probably just looking to get the holidays off for yourself."

He laughed. "That would be an expensive way to get a day off. No, this time of year is just another retail season for me. I usually work at the store on major holidays."

She raised an eyebrow. "No kidding?"

"I'm married to my work, and she's very demanding."

She looked out the window, blowing on the tea, but not actually drinking it. Her dark hair fell in waves past her shoulders. She had a freckle on the tip of her nose that he knew he'd kiss often if she were his girlfriend.

He took a long drink of his black coffee to chase away that idea. He couldn't date his assistant manager. Now he was torn over whether he really wanted her to take the job or not.

She looked at him and shrugged. "I don't have much of a choice. I just bought a condo that I'd rather not sell in this horrible market and I don't think I'm going to get a better offer."

"No need to sweet talk me." He tried to sound insulted, but couldn't hold back his pleasure. When had he smiled so often in the same day? Given what had happened in the last twelve hours, he should be frowning and swearing up a storm. "Why don't we head over there now? Then I'll call corporate and get the paperwork drawn up." He reached across the table and offered his hand. "And I forgot to mention the twenty-percent employee discount."

She glared at him, then sighed and shook his hand.

***

She followed him to the store—the very last place she wanted to be after the Night from Hell. Inside, several cashiers turned to look. From their smirks, she figured they'd watched the morning news, too.

In his office, she sat down across the desk from him. "What are my duties as assistant manager?" She'd pretty much handled everything at Sublime, but she'd never worked somewhere as big as Save Land. "Scheduling?" She tried not to frown. "Employee evaluations?" She might've groaned out loud; she wasn't sure.

He steepled his hands. "Tell me what your dream position would be."

Certainly not anything here, she thought. But she closed her eyes, thinking. She liked how Sublime was known as the most upscale boutique in town. It had an impeccable reputation. She liked the idea of image and branding, of making a mark on the community. But she also liked helping people. She opened her eyes. "What would you say Save Land's position is in the community?"

He laughed. "That isn't obvious? Big savings, 365 days a year."

She waved him off. "That's your slogan. I mean, how does the store fit in the community? What role do you play?"

He shrugged. "We're a place to save money."

"Do you offer grants? Scholarships? Do you host community events? Something for the holidays?" That's one thing she hadn't liked about Sublime. Maybe it could be different, here.

"We let the Salvation Army put their kettles outside the store." He turned up his hands. "We're just about saving money."

She uncrossed her legs and leaned forward. "I want to help Save Land make a mark in this community. I can't believe you don't have a toy drive for the holidays. Let me be in charge of community relations as assistant manager. That would be my dream job here." She smiled—probably for the first time all day.

He linked his hands behind his head, seemingly mulling over her idea. Was she pushing it? Was she going to be the new head of dressing room security instead?

Finally, he planted his elbows on his desk and smiled at her. "I think we can arrange that. Let's see how it goes, unofficially. Then I'll pitch the idea to corporate once we see how your plans work out for us."

She bit her lower lip; another old habit she couldn't break. "Really? That's great. Terrific."

"There's just one thing I should mention. Employees are required to wear clothing from the store while working. But you've got a head start with your new outfit."

The news hit her like a breakup. Her clothes. Her beautiful, expensive designer clothes—abandoned in her closet?! She felt her lip wobble. "Even the managers?"

He nodded.

She was quiet for a few moment, mourning the death of her style. Resigned, she sniffed. "I'll just get the leggings in every color."

"There's the Save Land spirit." He stood up and offered his hand. "Glad to you have you on board, Lindy."

She liked the feel of his hand in hers; and she liked that he didn't let go.

"And I should mention, company policy prohibits dating among employees."

She stepped back. "Of course. Right. Standard procedure at most places, right?" *Gotcha loud and clear.* She smoothed her shirt, trying to hide her embarrassment. *Was it that clear she was attracted to him?* "One more question. If employees wear store clothing, why are you decked out in Gucci?"

One eyebrow lifted. "Nice catch. It's a gift from an ex-girlfriend."

And why did that news buoy her heart just a bit? "So, it's okay for the boss to wear designer suits to work?"

"It seemed an appropriate choice when I learned I'd probably be on the news this morning talking about the missing woman's car found in our lot."

Her cheeks went hot. "Right."

"Speaking of which, I'd like to hold a press conference announcing we've hired you."

She groaned.

"We suffered some bad PR with you locked in overnight. We need to right that ship."

She straightened her shoulders. "That'll be the perfect time to announce the toy drive we're having." The idea had just come to her.

"Oh?"

She nodded. "The new assistant manager is going to stay locked in a dressing room until we fill a tractor trailer with new toys for charity." She raised her eyebrows. "Next Saturday."

He laughed. "Are you serious?"

With her hands on her hips she took a step forward and met his gaze. "As an emergency liquidation sale."

He whistled. "Well, then. Save Land has our first holiday fundraiser. Let me set up our press conference."

He was a step too close to her. He must've noticed it too, because he moved back. Then he clapped his hands together. "Why don't you hit the floor, introduce yourself and see how things work around here."

"I'll check on the dressing room procedures first."

Mr. Big Boss let out a nervous laugh.

***

He couldn't close the door behind her fast enough. Not only was she beautiful, she was smart, too, with some great ideas for the store. Maybe good enough to move up to store manger, so he could move on to a city with an adequate French restaurant. Hell, she'd probably be running the place in a month. So what was nagging the back of his mind now?

She reminded him of his old girlfriend, Zoe. They both had excellent taste in clothes—top of the line. He wondered if Lindy also had a shoe collection to rival the *Sex and the City* gals. Her face had gone practically white when he'd mentioned the dress code.

In the ten months he'd been in Rochester he hadn't dated anyone seriously. Zoe had laughed when he asked her if she wanted to move upstate with him. His instincts on her hadn't been so good. He spotted Lindy talking to the cashiers, uncertain what his instincts were telling him about *her*.

***

He looked up from the agenda Lindy had scrawled on a spiral notebook and blinked at her. "You want me to dress up like Santa next week?"

She nodded and her smile was so big he hated to break the news to her. "Lindy, I don't do holidays and I certainly don't do Santa."

She scrunched her eyebrows together. "What's that

54

supposed to mean?"

He shrugged. "Christmas has always been just another retail holiday for me. Even as a kid, my old man was at the store working so his employees could have the holiday off." In fact, his father worked day and night building Save Land into what it was today. That didn't make for much father-son bonding. Alex remembered exactly two basketball games during high school his father had been able to attend. And Alex had played horribly, being so nervous that his father was there. He sighed at the memory, but Lindy must have thought it was directed at her.

She pointed at him. "If I'm going to be wearing Save Land clothing forty hours a week, you can manage a Santa suit for a day."

He frowned. "I'll wear a red tie. That's the best I can do." He looked over her notes. "You think it's only going to take a day to fill up that truck?" He shook his head. "I think you're going to be holed up in that dressing room a lot longer than you were last night."

"I bet it gets filled before midnight Saturday."

He crossed his arms, intrigued—more than he should be. "What's the wager?"

She grinned. "A week of wearing whatever I want to the store."

"I've got several nice suits that haven't sent he light of day since I moved here. I'll take you up on that." He held his hand out, and she shook on it. And while he really wanted to pull her into his arms and discover how silky her hair felt against his cheek, how plump her lips really were, he knew he'd just have to settle for the feel of her small hand in his.

"It's a bet. That I'm going to win."

"Do you want to grab dinner?"

She raised her eyebrows.

"To talk about scheduling procedures," he said quickly. "Store policies"

She held a stack of files against her chest. "I've got a

lot of work to do tonight. I want to fine-tune a few ideas for community service programs before I pitch them to you."

He hadn't expected to feel so disappointed. "Great, that's great. Oh, and go pick out a new Save Land outfit to wear Monday morning during our press conference announcing our best hire in years. You haven't won that bet yet."

***

She drove home without remembering a moment of the ride. All she could think about was Alex's strong grip, the tiny scar by his right eye, those long dark lashes, and the way he smelled. He might be wearing Save Land's best casual wear, but he smelled like Armani.

She hung up her new Save Land outfit in the closet; kind of seemed like the new girl in school, hanging out with the snobby rich girls who won't give her the time of day. Much like her high school memories. She ran her fingers over the expensive fabric of her Dolce & Gabbana blazer and sighed. When would she have a chance to wear these beautiful clothes again?

She closed the closet door. It didn't matter. Within the past twenty-four hours, she'd been locked in a store, fired, and then hired to work in a totally new position. A crazy mix of emotions swirled inside her head. Add to that Alex's dinner invitation, and she was spinning. She fell back on her bed and stared up at lovely crystal chandelier she'd had installed. The shiny beads sparkled and winked at her. That's what she felt like inside, thinking about the future; thinking about Alex.

When she returned to work Monday morning, she had a list of ideas to share with him. "I want to host workshops, showing women how to put together the affordable pieces here at Save Land, but still making them look fashionable. And I'll show them how to mix and match their outfits to get more than one look."

He reached across the desk and touched her arm.

"Slow down, kiddo. What are you going to do the other 364 days of the year?"

She wondered if she was blushing. "I'm just excited about the opportunity. More excited than I could've imagined." Helping women with limited budgets look good just seemed more fulfilling than helping a socialite pick out three pricey dresses—one of which she *might* wear to the charity ball of the week.

"I can't wait to see what you do. Let's focus on the toy drive first. But before that, we've got a press conference to do." He reached for her hand and pulled her up from her chair.

"I'd rather be locked in the dressing room again. And by the way, you really need to upgrade the carpet in there."

***

Despite her nerves, the press conference was a hit, and the news crews promised to follow up that weekend and cover their toy drive.

When they got back to Alex's office, he high-fived her and set his hands on her shoulders. "That was great. You were great."

Her hands slid up his arms and she looked into his gray eyes. They both realized they were practically embracing. *We shouldn't be doing this.* Reluctantly, she stepped back. "Thanks," she said.

"You look great in the turtle-neck dress," he said. "I bet we sell out of those this week, now that you've modeled them for the cameras."

"I always pictured myself in Dior when I made my TV debut." She shrugged.

He stared at her, saying nothing, until she became so self-conscious she looked at her shoes. He hadn't mentioned having to wear Save Land shoes, so she had on her favorite Pradas. She looked up at him. "I've got to get everything ready for this weekend." She walked to the door.

"Lindy?"

She turned to him. "Yes?"

"I'm so glad you took the job. I really am."

***

The trailer was half-filled by noon on Saturday. Alex was impressed. Lindy had contacted radio stations and recruited local celebrities to stop by and encourage people to drop off toys. They'd set her up with a remote microphone in the dressing room, where they interviewed her from time to time, and gave her updates on the donation status.

He hadn't worn his Santa costume; a black Italian wool suit with a holiday-themed tie was festive enough for him, as he greeted the folks stopping by. It was a beautiful winter day, with a clear blue sky and snow glistening in the bright sun.

Inside, business was booming. The holidays were always busy, but the store was packed with people buying toys to donate, or shopping after they'd dropped off their gifts. Even his workers were in cheerier moods, some wearing Santa hats and antlers to join in the holiday fun. They all were crazy about Lindy.

He knew how they felt.

He grabbed a bag of chips and a soda to bring to her. She'd brought an e-reader, her iPod, and a pillow. "Those dressing rooms aren't made for sleeping," she'd told him.

A big wreath hung on the door, and he rapped softly. "You awake in there?"

The door unlocked, and she smiled at him, with a half-eaten candy cane in one hand. "You here to pay up on your bet?"

He smiled. "The trailer's not full yet. But look, I did even better than a red tie. It's got Christmas trees on it. How's that for festive?"

She smoothed her hand down his tie. "You would've looked cute in the Santa suit."

He decided to take that as a compliment. "Can I come in? I brought gifts."

She stepped back. "You can try. It's not exactly built for two."

Good. That meant he'd be close to her. He squeezed through the door and closed it behind him. "I've got snacks in case you're hungry."

"Thanks." She took a long gulp of the soda. "Sounds like we're getting a good turn out." Her smile was adorable.

"Yeah. And the gal from the Salvation Army wants to know if you'd help distribute the toys the week before Christmas."

Her eyes widened as she set her hand over her heart. "Really? That would be amazing." You'd think he'd told her she was getting this season's entire Blahnik collection for Christmas.

"I'll let her know."

She squeezed his arm. "I want you to come with me when we hand out the toys."

He opened and closed his mouth. He didn't want to go but he didn't want to say no.

She sat on the blanket she had spread on the floor, and he wished she were still touching him. He sat beside her. "I don't know about that..." Although, it would mean spending more time with her.

Her nicely manicured hand rested on his. "Please? It'll be fun. Just think about it. You're going to make some lucky kids' Christmas dreams come true. You have no idea how important it can be. It's something you remember forever. I still do." Her eyes widened and she looked away from him.

"What do you mean?"

She looked up at the ceiling and sighed. "My mom died when I was little. That Christmas, I got tons of toys from a local charity. Of course, I didn't know it at the time. I thought it was Santa's way of making it up to me. It made me believe I hadn't been forgotten. It was the only good thing that happened to me that year. I secretly thought it was a miracle." She pressed her eyes closed.

He drew in a breath and curled his hand around hers. "I'm so sorry you lost your mother."

She looked down and sniffed, her voice softening. "Being excited about toys probably sounds stupid after losing her," she said. "It wasn't just toys, though. It was more than that. It was hope that good things could still happen even after the very worst thing in the world happened."

She still wouldn't look at him. So Alex raised her chin with one finger and pressed his lips against hers, then pulled back. "It's not stupid at all. I'm glad you have a special memory like that. I never had reason to be excited for the holidays." He kissed her again. "But you're changing my mind about that. You're my holiday rush."

With that, she kissed him back, her arms on his shoulders, pulling him closer to her. Then she leaned back, as if she just realized what they were doing. "I'm sorry."

"I'm not."

"This has to be some sort of company violation."

"Locking you in a dressing room was too, but here we are doing that again."

She laughed and wiped away a tear. Then her phone rang. "That's the radio station. I've gotta take it."

He stood up, taking on his business tone again. "I need to get back to the truck." He paused before he slipped out the door. "I'll come with you to hand out those toys, Lindy."

She beamed at him and he knew that look would stay with him for a long time.

***

At eight-thirty, the tractor-trailer was only ninety-percent stocked with toys. But as far as Alex was concerned, the fundraiser was a huge success. The charity director was thrilled. But Lindy refused to come out until it was completely filled, even if that meant spending another night in the dressing room.

She deserves another miracle, he thought to himself. He pulled one of the cashiers from her post, and the two of them wheeled carts back to the toy section. "Fill yours with stuff for girls. I'll get toys for the boys."

He tossed in trucks and action figures, board games and building sets. Then he filled two more carts. He was flushed and excited as he loaded the toys onto the belt in the checkout line, just imagining Lindy's delight when she learned she'd reached her goal. "Don't tell Lindy about this," he told the cashier and the workers helping him. He was going to tell the charity director it'd been an anonymous donation. Because it had been.

Best twelve hundred dollars he'd ever spent.

***

Lindy checked the time on her cell phone. It was a quarter to nine and the store would be closing soon. She sighed. Looked like she'd be spending another night in the least likely of places. She leaned back against the wall. At least it was for a good cause. Some little kid would believe in miracles because of this.

She sat up with a start when someone rapped on the changing room door. "Can I come in?" It was Alex.

She jumped up and opened the door for him. He did look cute in his Christmas tie. She couldn't help but grin, while her heart fluttered, remembering how they'd kissed when he'd visited before.

He stepped inside. "Good news. An anonymous donor just dropped off enough toys to fill up the truck. You're outta here, kid!"

She stared at him for a moment, then threw her arms around him. He squeezed back tightly. Resting her check against his chest, she breathed in the smell of him.

He laughed, and caught her lips with his. "We shouldn't be doing this," she said between kisses.

"Shh."

Then she looked up at him and whispered, "Thanks."

"For kissing you?"

She slugged him softly. "For letting me do the toy drive."

"You're incredible. You're thanking me for letting you collect toys for needy kids? You're right. We should've been doing this all along."

She slid her hands down his chest and stepped back. "Just part of my job."

He looked away and cleared his throat. "Come on, get your stuff so we can go see the truck and go out and celebrate."

"And don't forget, I get to wear whatever I want for a week."

He faked a frown. "I almost forgot about that."

***

After pictures with the newspaper and interviews with TV and radio stations, Lindy climbed into Alex's car and they went out for a drink. It was exactly like she'd imagined her blind date with Spencer would've been: sitting close, lots of flirty comments, and a tightness in her tummy that hummed. But this was her boss, the guy who'd just given her a job. What if things went badly between the two of them? She couldn't go crawling back to Sublime.

Afterward, when he dropped her off at her car in the parking lot, he kissed her again; this time with a passion that could start steaming the windows. "Good night," she whispered, slipping out the door before that kiss could become something more.

But she didn't stop thinking about him all night. *Can't have everything, sister.*

***

"What's up with you?" Darcy asked over coffee and croissants the next morning. "I thought you'd be devastated working at Save Land, but you're so…" She frowned, looking for the words. "You're so happy. What gives?"

Lindy set down her coffee cup on their kitchen

table and settled her chin in her hand. She hadn't realized how much Darcy had thrived on her disheveled life. But it wasn't like that anymore. Lindy found herself smiling in the morning and whistling when she came home from work. Whistling! Lindy was not a whistler.

Darcy snapped her fingers. "Earth to Lindy."

"Sorry. I'm just..." She sighed. "I'm great. Work's good. I love the holidays and..." She snapped her mouth shut. She wasn't going to tell Darcy how she felt about Alex. Her crush would have to run its course; there was nowhere for it to go.

She pushed away from the table and headed to the store even though it was her day off. Alex was there, and she wanted to talk about plans for her fashion workshops. Yeah, that's why she wanted to see him.

***

They were scheduled to deliver toys the Saturday before Christmas. She arrived at the charity warehouse and scanned the big room packed with boxes. She didn't see Alex. The charity director was there and some other people, along with a Santa, but no Alex. Had he forgotten?

Wringing her hands, she wondered how long she'd wait for him before leaving. That's when Santa headed her way. "Ho, ho, ho, little girl. Have you been naughty or nice this year?"

Her jaw dropped. "Alex?" She stepped back, taking in his red velvet glory. It wasn't a cheapie Santa suit, either, but an expensive, gorgeous costume with thick fur and beautifully detailed buttons. His shiny black boots were made of real leather.

She tugged at his curly beard. "You look great. Too bad they don't have Mrs. Santa suits at Save Land. I could've dressed up with you."

He raised a whitewashed eyebrow. "You're not the first person to ask for a Mrs. Santa suit from Save Land. But luckily, I picked one up at the costume shop for you."

She planted her hands on her hips. "And how did you know my size?"

"I've worked in retail my whole life. I can spot a six when I see one."

She knew she was blushing, especially with the way he was surveying her size-six shape. "Thank you. Let me go change." She grabbed the costume and dashed to the bathroom. After changing, she did a quick twirl in the mirror, pleased with her holiday transformation.

Alex rubbed his belly appreciatively when she came out. "Looking good Mrs. Santa. Or is it Miss?"

She adjusted the tie on her apron. "I met a lovely gent online, but that kind of fell through." She narrowed her eyes at him.

"Well, maybe Santa will come through with a new beau for you." He held out his arm for her. "Shall we?"

***

Alex couldn't believe how much fun he was having. Some families opted to have their gifts discreetly delivered so they could surprise the kids Christmas morning. Others had decided to get their gifts early. The Johnsons were one of those families. Alex transferred the contents of their donation box into his big canvas sack, then he and Lindy dashed up the creaky steps of the duplex and rang the bell for the lower apartment.

A little blond-haired girl peeked out the door. Her eyes widened. "Mommy, Mommy! Santa's here early! And he brought Mrs. Clause! Hurry!" She jumped and twirled and clapped waiting for her mom. Alex tried to remember when he'd ever seen someone so happy.

A short, thin woman opened the door and smiled, though it didn't quite reach her eyes. "Hello, Mr. And Mrs. Clause! Please come in."

The moment Alex stepped in, the little girl latched her arms around his legs. His throat tightened and he struggled to swallow.

Luckily, Lindy spoke up. "Are you Madison Monahan?"

The little girl nodded enthusiastically.

Lindy clasped her hands in front of her. "Oh, good. Santa and I are doing some early deliveries. We're so busy on Christmas, you know, and we wanted to be certain we got presents to some very special children, like you."

Madison's eyes were wide and she tucked in her lips, not saying a word, lest she break the magical spell that they all seemed to be under

Alex knelt beside her and opened his bag. "These are all for you." He did his best to make his voice sound deep and jolly.

Madison's jaw dropped and she fell to her knees. She looked at the presents, then looked up at her mother. "See? I told you Santa wouldn't forget us. You said Santa might not come this year but you were wrong." She grabbed a present, and stared at the big gift tag that read, "To Madison, From Santa." She hugged it, holding it tight against her chest. She started tearing open the package, when she paused. "Santa, did you bring anything for Mommy?"

Alex looked at Lindy, who subtly shook her head no. Then inspiration struck. "That's so thoughtful to think of your mommy. I'm glad you reminded me. It's out in the—it's outside." He held up a finger. "I'll be right back."

He slipped out the door and unlocked his car. His wallet was stuffed in the glove compartment, and he fished out four fifty-dollar gift cards to Save Land. Dashing back inside he smiled at Lindy and her questioning look. "Mrs. Monahan, these are for you."

"It's Miss," she said, softly. "But thank you. Thank you so much." She looked at the gift cards, and swiped the back of her hand along her cheek.

Madison looked up from the doll she was struggling to free from its plastic prison. "We're not married anymore. Daddy left and it's really sad. All the time." She reached for another present.

Lindy's hand hovered over her throat. She bent down next to the girl and stroked her hair. "Things will get better, honey. Don't ever give up hope."

Madison beamed up at her. "I won't, Mrs. Clause."

***

Lindy broke down when they got into his car. Alex reached for her. "That must bring back a lot of memories."

She nodded. "I'm sorry. I shouldn't be crying." She tried to fake a laugh through her tears, but he knew she was bluffing.

He brushed a finger along her cheekbone, catching a tear. "That girl will always remember this Christmas, just like you did. Me, I don't remember any. We didn't go to church. Didn't decorate beyond a simple tree. Sure, there were presents, but nothing I can remember to this day. I bet you remember every present you got that Christmas."

She nodded and laughed for real this time. "Four dolls—one which peed when you gave it a bottle. A stroller and high chair for the dolls. Doll clothes, too." She stared out the window, and he bet she could still see the toys. "Art supplies, two teddy bears, and an etch-a-sketch." She looked at him and smiled with a shrug.

He turned the car on. "And she'll remember, too. Come on. We've got a few more houses to hit." He wasn't sure how he was going to do it, but Alex knew he had to make this a Christmas to remember for Lindy.

***

When they finished delivering the gifts, Alex invited her back to his place. She hesitated, but she wasn't ready for their day to end. "I think I missed my calling," she said.

"How so?"

"I've spent so long working with the wealthiest clientele, and a big commission day is awesome, but today? It's one of the happiest days I've had in a long

66

time. I think someday I'd like to open a thrift shop with great, affordable merchandise, so I can really reach out to people like Madison and her mom. Maybe I could even offer sewing classes, and teach them how to embellish their clothes." She clasped her hands, just thinking of it.

"They're not going to appreciate your designer wardrobe."

She shrugged. "I'll save it for special occasions."

"What do you say we go out for dinner tonight, and you can wear one of your favorite Chanels?"

She tipped her head. "That would be great."

***

He wasn't planning to see his folks until after Christmas, so he was surprised to see his father's number show up on his cell two days before Christmas.

"Alex, what the hell's going on up there?"

"Happy holidays to you, too, Dad."

He laughed. "Right. And I hear that holiday sales have been very happy in your neck of the woods. Your numbers are great. And this new assistant manager is doing some good work. I'm impressed with the publicity she's garnered for the store."

Alex grinned to himself. Pleased, not that he'd salvaged a potential PR nightmare with the dressing room incident, but that Lindy's ideas had caught his father's attention—a tough old coot to impress.

"So, here's an early holiday gift for you, son. Your stint in Rochester is up. Promote that gal to manager, and take your pick of stores. Get back to me after the holidays with your decision."

Alex said nothing for a moment, then, "Right. Of course, thanks, Dad."

He held on to the phone for a while after his father hung up. He wasn't sure how he felt, but he knew he had to see her. He didn't know what her plans were for Christmas—he was working the night shift, she was working the morning—but he didn't want to wait to share the news. Would she be pleased by the promotion?

Of course she will. More money, she's in charge again. But what did this mean for them? He took a chance and stopped by her place.

When she opened the door, she was wearing sweats. Not what he'd expected, but cute nonetheless. Her eyes went wide.

He reached for her arm. "Don't worry. It's good news. I've got an early Christmas gift for you."

She grinned. "Ooh, I like presents. Come in." She led him to the family room and sat down. Her teacup yorkie hopped on her lap and a blonde stuck her head in from the kitchen.

"Darcy, this is my boss, Alex."

"The one who nearly gave me a heart attack by locking you in the dressing room?"

"That would be the one," Lindy said.

Darcy crossed her arms. "I should have scored a gift card out of the deal, too. I was a wreck."

Alex reached in his wallet and handed over a fifty-dollar gift card. Darcy snatched it and giggled. "Thanks! I'll leave you two alone." Her mood had instantly lifted and she put on her coat and slipped out the door. "I'll do a little last minute shopping with this."

Lindy rolled her eyes. "Sorry about her. Hope that wasn't my present she ran off with." She laughed.

He set his hand on her knee. "It's a little better than a gift card. I heard from my father today and he wants to promote you to manager of the Rochester Save Land."

She suppressed a chuckle. "That's really nice of your dad, but maybe you have to clear this with your boss?"

He looked at her, and realized she wasn't kidding. She didn't know who he was. They had this 'thing' between them and she didn't know who he was? His chest tightened in a way he hadn't felt before. Had anyone ever wanted him—just for him and not his fortune or his name?

He took her hand and squeezed. "Lindy, my dad is my boss. He started the Save Land chain forty years ago."

Her eyebrows shot up. "Oh, my God. I'm so sorry. I didn't know who you were." She smacked her hand on her forehead. "You must think I'm the biggest idiot. Like, deserving-of-a-crown idiot." She tickled her dog's chin. "Bitsy here probably even knew who you were." She let out a long sigh.

"I'm thrilled you didn't know who I am. I thought maybe..." He shook his head. She wasn't like Zoe, not at all. "But really. He wants to move you up to manager after the holidays."

She rubbed her dog's ears, probably a bit too hard. It yelped and jumped off the couch. "And what about you?" she asked.

He pressed his lips together. "My dad will transfer me wherever I want to go."

She shook her head. "I don't want you to leave." She closed her eyes and her voice dropped to a whisper. "I'd miss you too much. I won't take it."

He hadn't expected this; but he was thrilled. "We can't be a couple if we're both working there, Lindy."

"And we can't be a couple if you're not living here. It just won't work." She looked down and sniffed. "And I thought this was going to be a great Christmas."

He put his arm around her. "It's not Christmas yet, honey. We'll figure something out." He stood up and headed for the door.

"Where are you going?"

"I need to find you another Christmas present now, don't I?"

Her jaw dropped as he opened the door.

"I won't disappoint. I promise." He knew exactly how he was going to give her another Christmas miracle.

***

Lindy hated to cry, but here she was crying again

for the third time in a month. She sighed. Was she only allowed professional or personal happiness? Not both at the same time? There didn't seem to be a solution here. They couldn't be a couple and keep working together. And if she took the job, he was gone. Feeling too sick to eat dinner, she went to bed early, certain Santa wouldn't show up in a few days with a way to make it all better. That was only fairy tale stuff for kids. Because no matter what gift Alex showed up with, she wouldn't be able to have what she wanted—him.

She woke up without the close-to-Christmas thrill she usually had this time of year. She didn't want her mood to rub off on the shoppers, so she donned a Santa hat, dressed in a red sweater from Save Land, and brought along a mug of peppermint hot cocoa.

The number of shoppers rushing in for last minute gifts, or extra party supplies surprised her. Why did everyone wait until the last minute? She always had gifts purchased and wrapped weeks ahead of time. Sometimes months. The store was busy enough that she manned a register next to Gloria, one of her favorite cashiers.

During a lull in business, they took a fifteen-minute break and headed back to the lunchroom. Gloria popped open a soda. "Sure is nice having you on board, Lindy."

She grinned. "Thanks. It wasn't the most auspicious beginning, but I'm happy here." *But will I be if Alex leaves?*

Gloria took a long drink. "We all had a bet on how long you'd last."

Lindy planted her hands on her hips, but Gloria set her soft hand on Lindy's arm. "We've all taken our money back. The bet's off. We're keeping you. And the boss is pretty happy with you, too."

Lindy just knew she was blushing.

"Mercy, when he bought six carts full of toys to fill up that trailer of yours, we didn't know what happened to our boss." Her eyebrow cocked up.

Lindy placed her hand on her chest. "What?" she whispered.

Gloria's smile fell. "Shoot. I wasn't supposed to tell you that." Gloria checked her watch. "Time to get back to work." She hustled out of the break room before Lindy could ask any more questions.

Still stunned, Lindy wandered back to the manager's office; Alex's office. She dropped into a chair and stared at the ceiling, wondering what to make of this news.

The door opened and she looked up. It was Alex. "You alright?" he asked.

Her hands circled in the air as she searched for the words. "The toys. You bought all those toys."

Alex frowned. "I never should have scheduled you and Gloria together. She gets the word out faster than Twitter."

"Why did you do it?"

He walked over to her and knelt beside her. "So you didn't have to spend another night in the changing room." He slid his hand on her shoulder. "So your idea would be a success. So you could wear whatever you wanted for a week."

She leaned her head against him. "Thank you. For someone who says he doesn't have the Christmas spirit, you certainly came through."

"And then there's this." He handed her a box. "Since the promotion wasn't such a hit."

She pulled the ribbon off the gold box and lifted the lid. She gasped. "The Hermes scarf from Sublime! I was saving up for that." She clapped her hands like a little girl.

"I know. You mentioned that when you were telling me off for losing your job."

She felt her cheeks burning. "Sorry. My priorities were a little different back then."

"Speaking of which, there's one more thing. Get

your coat on." He stood up and held out his hand.

"What if it gets busy?"

"The second shift is filing in now. We won't be gone long."

She followed him, knowing she was just making this worse. They didn't have a future, and she was falling harder for him each moment.

He led her to his car, and they drove to an empty plaza a few miles away. He parked the car and leaned over to kiss her.

Nose-to-nose, she giggled. "You brought me all this way to kiss me?"

"That's just a bonus. I brought you here to show you your other gift."

Her laugh bubbled out. "What do you mean?"

"See that store right there?"

She followed his gesture and looked at the empty storefront with a for rent sign in the window. "Yes…."

His grin was huge. "It's yours. I rented it for you for six months. Now you can open that thrift store you were talking about and I'll stay at Save Land."

Her heart was stuck in her throat. "Seriously?" she whispered. "You're staying?"

He nodded. "Unless you don't want me to." His face paled a bit.

She grabbed his hand. "Of course I want you to stay." She shook her head and sighed. "I never thought another Christmas could match that one when I was five." She looked over at the store, then back at him. "I can't believe it." She squeezed his hand. "Thank you for helping me believe in holiday magic again."

"And thank you for helping me find it for the first time." He leaned over and kissed her again, slow and soft this time. On cue, the snow started to swirl down in big, downy flakes. "I hope this means you're resigning," he said.

"It'll be hard to give up the employee discount, but I'm going to have to go." She smiled at him, happier than she could remember. It'd only taken Santa twenty years, but two days before Christmas, he'd come though with another miracle for her—wrapped up in a six-foot tall blond bow and a gorgeous Armani winter coat.

"Missing Christmas"
By Lisa Scott

Before dashing off for work, Ryan came back to the bedroom and kissed me goodbye. "Two days until Christmas, Ginny. Are you excited?"

Normally when the holiday was that close I'd be up early, wearing musical antlers and doing improvised ballet moves to The Nutcracker while baking cookies. Instead, I was snoozing in bed. I sat up. "Yeah, really excited," I lied.

It might as well have been two hundred days until Christmas. Living in Florida after spending my whole life up north, the days down here all seemed the same. But, I'd only been here a month. Maybe that feeling would change.

"I'm looking forward to it, too. These sixty-hour weeks are killing me. Can't wait to take the day off and just hang out with you. Have a great day, babe." He kissed me again and left.

The house was empty and quiet without Ryan, and I faced another long day alone. I'd already unpacked our things, cleaned the house and the garage, and rearranged our furniture three times. I was running out of things to do until I found a job.

I fell back asleep and the doorbell rang, which was strange. I hadn't made any new friends here yet. Every time I told my girlfriends back home things were just awesome, I was lying. I couldn't tell them I might have made the biggest mistake of my life moving away from Rochester and everything—and everyone—I knew.

I peeked out the front window to see who was there. A delivery truck idled in my driveway. Hopefully it wasn't baked goods from my mother; that was possibly the only good thing about moving down here—avoiding her cooking.

"Hi, there," I said, opening the door.

"Good morning. Are you Ginny McDonald?

I nodded.

"I've got a delivery for you. Sign here, please."
The deliveryman handed me a clipboard and I scrawled
my signature before taking the cardboard box from him
that, sadly, was just the right size for a few fruitcakes and
a bunch of unpalatable cookies. I crossed my fingers,
hoping for cute shoes instead. "Thanks!"

My neighbor next door saw me and waved. She
stopped watering her flowers and wandered over to my
porch. "Beautiful day, huh? Aren't you two going to
decorate for Christmas?" I noticed she was wearing a T-
shirt with a picture of a glowing Christmas light on front
and the caption 'Christmas Turns Me On.'

She saw me inspecting her shirt and looked down at
it. "You like it? It glows in the dark. The gentlemen
down at the senior center think it's a hoot."

"It's great." I'd only talked with Edna twice, but in
those short visits she'd informed me she was a widow
from Michigan who'd moved down to Florida after her
husband died, thrilled to make their winter home her
permanent residence. Oh, and she didn't have children,
but she did have two little Shih Tzus who yapped at the
mourning doves that roosted in our backyard and we
were to pay them no mind, unless they got into our
garbage, in which case we were allowed to squirt them
with the hose.

Holding my box, I forced a smile. "It just seems
weird to decorate when there's no snow."

She waved her hand in dismissal. "Nonsense. I put
out more decorations down here *because* there's no snow.
My husband and I never got up all our lights since it was
always too darn cold outside. This is just lovely." She
smiled up at the sun, and then looked at me. "So, you
haven't found a job yet?"

Great. She was one of those kinds of neighbors.
"Um, no. You know how bad the economy is." I'd
applied to four bakeries in town, but no one was hiring.
I'd even looked for a seasonal position at the local Save

Land, but they'd finished all their Christmas hiring already. So, I kept myself busy unpacking and setting up our new house. I'd moved around the pictures in the family room four times. Ryan hadn't noticed when I showed him. "Just decorate however you want, Gin. I'll leave that up to you. You do a real good job with that."

Edna planted her hands on her hips. "Well, you must be glad you aren't up in Rochester. Heard on TV a big storm's headed that way." She made a disapproving face, like the residents had voted on having a holiday blizzard.

"Really? I better check that out."

She planted her hands on her hips. "Must've been tough moving away from your family. I would've missed my Mama too much. Good for you, you brave thing."

I plastered on a great big smile. "Yep. That's me. Brave Ginny. Well, have a Merry Christmas if I don't see you."

"Oh, I'll see you. I'm stopping by tomorrow with a fruitcake for you." She nodded after delivering that bit of good news.

I gulped. "Awesome."

She started back toward her house, then turned around. "I didn't notice a ring on your finger. Aren't you two engaged?"

Out came another fake smile. "Not yet. We've been together less than a year."

Her eyes widened. "And you moved all the way down here with him?"

I hugged the box against me. "Love will do that to you, right?"

"I suppose it does. Well, I'll see you kids later." With a wave, she returned to her house.

I stood on the porch, staring at my package. I'd spent three minutes with the woman and she'd picked up on one of the things niggling at my heart. Ryan and I had talked about getting married, but he'd told me, "I'm not ready yet."

That was reasonable, I'd thought. We hadn't been together that long, but my friend Harper had warned me not to move down here without a ring. "I've read some statistics about the percentage of women who get married after living with a guy, and the numbers aren't pretty."

"We've only been dating ten months!" I'd argued. "Maybe I'm not ready."

"I'm just sharing the research," Harper had said.

I reminded myself that studies weren't always right and went inside, setting the box on the kitchen table. I ran a knife through the tape on each side. The scent of pine hit me, and for a moment I worried Mom had come up with some new crazy cookie recipe. Then I pulled out the tissue paper wrapped around a gorgeous holiday arrangement. Boughs of pine formed a cute little basket, and it was filled with pinecones, cinnamon sticks, clementines, and berries. I opened the card nestled inside.

"Dear Ginny,

Hope Florida is treating you well. Your moving down South to chase love got me to pluck up my courage and take a few chances of my own. I'll tell you all about it next time I see you. Just wanted to send along one of the new arrangements I'm making at the florist shop to say thanks. These have been a big hit. Chelsea and I will be missing you at your mom's party. Love and kisses, Marnie."

I set the basket on the kitchen table and admired Marnie's work. It was great she was finally getting over her divorce. I'd somehow inspired her? That was shocking. Good thing she didn't know how uncertain I was feeling now. Then, remembering Edna's news about the storm, I hustled over to the TV and turned on the Weather Channel.

"The snow is flying in Rochester, New York, and folks here can expect a foot or more of the white stuff in the next twenty-four hours. A winter storm watch is in effect until Christmas Eve." The forecaster sounded way too chirpy to be delivering news of a holiday storm. Her snowflake earrings swung like pendulums as she turned to the camera with a grin. "Looks like they won't have to dream of a white Christmas—they'll have one, guaranteed."

I flicked off the TV and went out into the backyard. Truthfully, I was jealous. I loved hunkering down and waiting for a storm to cover the ground in a fresh coat of white while I nestled inside under a blanket with a mug of cocoa and a good book. Howling wind and driving snow only made me feel that much cozier. Even better was snuggling up with Ryan during a storm. It just wasn't the same in an air-conditioned room on a balmy night. After so much complaining about shoveling and bundling up in the winter, I'd had no idea how much I would miss it.

I closed my eyes, trying to imagine I was back home, but a bead of sweat trickled down the side of my face, bringing me back to face the eighty-five-degree day. I padded across the lawn, the thick grass rough on my feet, and sat down under the shade of our big orange tree. No oranges yet, but the realtor had promised it always yielded a bumper crop. Maybe I could make marmalade. Fresh-squeezed orange juice would be nice, too, right?

Ryan wouldn't be home from work for another five hours. Sure, it was two days until Christmas and most everyone else had the day off, but he was the newbie, so he got stuck working the holiday week. His job as a lineman for the electric company had brought us down here from Rochester. We'd moved the day after Thanksgiving. He'd made a bunch of new friends at work and was completely in love with the Sunshine State. I hated complaining, ruining his happiness with his new situation.

"Why are you so quiet, honey?" he'd asked me more than once in the past few weeks. I'd tried telling him I was having a hard time adjusting, but he dismissed the idea, telling me to be patient since we'd just gotten here.

I whistled for Hershey, Ryan's chocolate Lab, who was rooting around in the corner of our yard. Her ears perked up and she bounded over with something dangling from her mouth.

I leaned forward for a closer look and screamed; it was a snake. "Hershey, drop it!" No way was she bringing that thing inside.

She looked at me and cocked her head.

"Drop it!"

Like a reluctant kid, she released it, then batted it around with her paw. For a moment, I thought it was dead, but then it slithered away. I wasn't going to wait around for it to come back, so I dashed back inside, Hershey hot on my heels, and locked the door behind me. I was breathing hard, trying to convince myself I'd get used to all the critters down here. I'd grown fond of the little lizards that crept along the side of our house, but all the snakes and bugs? Not so much.

I flung open the freezer door to get a container of ice cream, but we were out. *Hadn't I just bought four pints earlier this week?* They were disappearing quickly these days. Hopefully, Ryan wouldn't be looking for one when he came home. It'd be embarrassing having to explain *that*. Well, it was that or cookies—pick your poison.

A big black bug scuttled across the kitchen floor and I reminded myself to call the exterminator. Palmetto bugs, that's what Ryan told me they were, and apparently as common as house flies. Oh, so much adjusting for me to do.

I slipped on my flip-flops, because stepping on one of those things barefoot would put me over the edge. After scooting out of the kitchen, I started unloading the clothes from the dryer, wondering how to pass the rest of the day until Ryan finished work. Back home, Mom and my older sister, Gretchen, were probably humming along to holiday music while they pulled out and cleaned the fancy china and crystal pieces for the Christmas blowout my parents hosted every year. Usually it took the entire score of The Nutcracker Suite to finish the job.

I wondered who'd string the fresh garland on the staircase. That was always my job. Every year, we'd go to the Christmas tree farm and pick out an eight-foot tree, chop it down, and drag it through the woods. Then we'd cut off the bottom two feet and use the boughs for the garland. Later, we'd congratulate ourselves with board games and eggnog. I was the reigning queen of Monopoly in our family. Gretchen always insisted I cheated—she suspected I smuggled in Monopoly money from another game set to pad my bank account—but she was just a sore loser. I'm sure my elaborate victory dances didn't help her mood, either.

I folded the last of the towels from the dryer and opened the storage closet in the hall, where I'd stashed the Christmas village pieces I'd collected over the years. I'd been enchanted with my grandmother's set when I was a little girl, so every year she'd given me a new piece for Christmas. Mom picked up the tradition after Grandma died. I had a good-sized village by now, and I'd been meaning to put them on the banquet table Ryan had bought just for the occasion. So far, I hadn't been motivated to set it all up.

I pulled out the box with my favorite Victorian building: the toyshop with a big bay window in front and little toys on a workbench. Santa and his elves were at work inside, swinging hammers and slinging saws. Ryan had been bugging me to put out the village since we'd hauled it down with us. But I put the toyshop back in the box; I still wasn't in the mood.

I wandered out to the family room and flopped on the couch, hugging a pillow on my lap. The neighbor's yard across the street caught my eye. They'd decorated their two palm trees with white lights, and had even brought in a crane so they could string the lights all the way to the top. It looked beautiful at night, but it felt more like I was staying at a tropical resort than counting down to the holidays.

Ryan had bought us an artificial tree and put it up one night after work. He'd even handled the lights since I hated doing that, but I'd only hung up half the new ornaments we'd bought. I'd been waiting for it to feel like the holidays, but that hadn't happened so far.

My cell rang and I answered it. My niece, Isabelle, was crying. "Aunt Ginny? We need you! Grandma burned our gingerbread men." She was nine and took our holiday baking very seriously. Every year we made gingerbread men—one for each person in the family, decorated to look like them more or less—and distributed them on Christmas day. "The outsides of the people are all crispy black and the insides are still gooey." Isabelle sniffed on the other end of the line. "They're not like yours."

That brought an instant lump to my throat. "Oh, honey. I'm so sorry. You can make another batch, can't you? Let me talk to Grandma."

"Okay. Tell her how to make them the right way."

I heard rustling as Isabelle handed the phone off to my mother.

"How are you, darling?" Mom asked. "You lucky thing. It's probably hot and sunny down there and we're getting a boatload of snow."

My throat tightened at the sound of her voice and I tried hard not to sound emotional. "I'm good. Great." I faked a smile for my own benefit. "It's real nice here today."

I couldn't let her know how sad I was feeling. Ryan and I had only been together ten months, and she'd warned me it was too soon to move across the country with him. My job at the bakery in town hadn't been reason enough to stay in Rochester, so when he asked me if I would come with him, I said yes right away. I was worried a long-distance relationship wouldn't work. I loved him and didn't want to lose him.

But so far Ryan and I had bickered more than we ever had back home. The only time we'd ever fought when we were still in Rochester was standing in front of a Red Box kiosk, trying to decide what to rent. My friends had refused to double date with us because we were "too perfect." We'd finish each other's sentences and come up with a new pet name every week. I'd leave love notes on the front seat of his car. He'd bring me a treat every time he came to see me: a gourmet cookie from a rival bakery so I could check out the competition, a new herbal tea to try, a sweet card.

But so far down in Florida there'd been no treats or notes in the bustle of getting settled in. It seemed like we'd left some of the magic back up north. I guess it was the stress of living together for the first time—in an entirely new place.

Mom grumbled on the end of the line. "I'm not sure what I did wrong, but the kitchen's filled with smoke. Poor Rudy's been barking her head off with the fire alarm blaring." On cue, the dog let out a pitiful howl.

I knew exactly what she'd done wrong. Mom always thought you could cook things faster by raising the temperature and baking it for a shorter time. Needless to say, Dad or I cooked most of the meals at home, and everyone else brought dishes to pass on the holidays. But Mom was good at other things, as she liked to remind us.

I squeezed the bridge of my nose. "Mom, what temperature did you bake them at?"

Silence. Then, "Four hundred fifty degrees for ten minutes."

I groaned. "Mom, you have to bake them at three hundred fifty degrees for twenty minutes."

"I thought this way would be quicker." She sounded offended that her reasoning hadn't worked. Then she sighed. "It's just that we have so many to make. And the girls are so impatient." Another sigh. "I wish you were here."

I looked up at the ceiling, hoping to stop my tears. "Me, too. I heard a storm's on the way. I hope everyone will be able to make it to the party." Everyone except for me, that is.

"Nonsense, everyone will be here. It's nothing that a four-wheel drive can't handle. Here, Brooke wants to talk to you now. Love you and miss you like crazy, kiddo."

"You too, Mom."

More shuffling of the phone, then Brooke got on the line, with her syrupy sweet, seven-year-old voice and her adorable lisp. "Aunt Ginny, what should we do with *your* cookie? We're going to make one for Ryan, too. Should we mail it? Or maybe Santa could deliver it to you. I could leave it out for him with a note."

Now I couldn't keep the tears back. "Save it for me, honey. Put it in a container so I can see it next time I'm home." I scrubbed the back of my hand along my cheek.

"And when will that be? Every time I come to Grandma's, I forget you're not going to be here. It's so sad. Christmas is not going to be fun without you. I bet no one else will give us piggyback rides."

I held the phone away from my mouth and let out a shuddering sob. Then I took a deep breath. "Now don't go on like that sweetie. I'm sure someone else will. You're going to have a great Christmas. And I'll see you real soon."

"But when?"

Good question. "I'm not sure."

"I hate Florida, even though that's where Disney is. So I like that part of Florida. I hate your part, though," she said.

I needed to change the topic. "How's school?"

She was quiet for a moment. "William Jacobs says I talk funny." She sniffed. "He laughs at me and tries to make his S's sound like mine. And then the other kids laugh, too."

My fists clenched and I wanted to tell her to slug him like I did when Nate Johnson had pulled my braids on the bus in second grade. But schools kind of look down on that these days. "Well, then William Jacobs must not be a nice little boy, and certainly won't be getting many presents from Santa this year. I love your special S's and I love everything about you." Oh, how I wished I were there to hug her.

"I love you everything about you, too. Except where you live. Okay, gotta go. We're having hot chocolate now. It bubbled up over the pan, but Grandma put a candy cane in it. Bye, Aunt Ginny."

"Bye, honey." I hung up before she could hear my sob-fest. What had I been thinking? I wasn't meant to be away from my family. They needed me. I guess twenty-three years of tradition trumped ten months of smitten, new love. Sending me down to Florida was like leaving a snowman out in the sun; I was slowly disappearing.

I wondered if a walk on the beach would help, maybe remind me of all the good things about living down south. Truly, it was gorgeous here and everyone seemed so happy. We lived about a mile from the beach, so I put on my sneakers and hoped the fresh sea air would boost my mood. I brought Hershey with me, along with a couple of tennis balls. At least she'd be having a good day.

I took off her leash and heaved a ball across the golden stretch of sand. A group of gulls scattered, totally put out by Hershey's arrival. Just a few people were on the beach, tucked under umbrellas, reading, or poking along the shore, looking for shells. I thought the lapping of the waves would calm me and make me grateful for the warm, lovely day.

But it didn't. It reminded me how much I wanted to be bundled up in a sweater, surrounded by the smell of fresh pine and roast turkey—my dad handled the latter. My phone rang again. I didn't know if I could deal with another call from my nieces.

It was my sister. "Ginny, how do you twist these stupid, prickly pieces of tree onto the banister!" She sounded like she was in pain.

"Ten years of practice, baby."

"No, really. It always looks so beautiful when you do it, and my garland looks like someone murdered a tree on the stairs. I wish you were here to help." She sighed. "I think we're going to go without the garland this year. So, are you busy decorating down there?"

I sniffed. "No, not yet. I'm at the beach right now."

"Don't rub it in!"

I lobbed a shell into the water. "Oh, it's just me and the dog. It's not that exciting."

"Why don't you do some baking?"

I shrugged, like she could see me. "I'm not really in the mood this year."

"Shut up. You are Martha Stewart's long-lost daughter, because you certainly didn't get that creativity from Mom. What's wrong? Aren't things going well?"

I wasn't ready to admit it to my sister just yet. "It's just been a bit harder than I thought."

Gretchen was quiet for a moment. "It'll get better, kiddo. Just give it time."

Inwardly, I groaned. If another person told me to give it more time, I might scream.

"It could be worse," she continued. "You could have needles stuck in your fingers and two kids begging to update their lists for Santa. Enjoy the peace and quiet."

I could hear the kiddos laughing in the background. "I'll try."

"Oh, your friends invited me to join them for their annual New Year's Eve night out. But I told them no way was I going to be a Ginny McDonald stand-in, like I'm one of the not-so-famous Kardashians showing up for Kim."

I tried to swallow, but couldn't. I forced a laugh. "New Year's with the girls was always fun." I'd be missing our St. Patrick's Day spa getaway, too. Instead of freezing our butts off at the parade, we'd spend the day at the spa and then go out later, joking around that we were sure to get lucky later that night. Never happened, but it was always a blast spending the day together.

"Well, talk to you on Christmas, Ginny. It won't be the same without you."

"But hey, maybe you'll win Monopoly this year." I hoped I sounded funnier than I felt. I tucked my phone in my pocket, took off my shoes, and stood in the foamy surf, letting the water wash over my feet. Hershey dropped her ball next to me, and started gnawing on a piece of driftwood. I stared across the water and realized how lonely I really was. Not just because Ryan was at work. I knew right then and there, this wasn't the place for me. Just like polar bears didn't thrive down south, neither did I.

I put the Hershey back on the leash and let her drag me home. Usually, I jogged ahead of her, but I was dreading going back to the house because deep down, I knew what I had to do; I had to leave. I couldn't do this anymore. I had to move home. I'd be suffering one hell of a broken heart, but I couldn't miss out on all those memories unfolding without me. Coming here had been a mistake. The phone calls from home made that clear. Once I got back to our cute little stucco ranch, I sorted through my dresser drawers and started packing. I grabbed my makeup, my flat iron—whatever I could cram into my two suitcases. Ryan would have to ship the rest to me. I teared up just thinking about it, but it was for the best.

I thought about leaving a note, but he deserved better than that. With a trembling hand, I dialed his cell, hoping he wasn't on top of a ladder when he answered. I held my breath while the phone rang, my throat growing tighter. By the time he answered, all I could do was cry into my cell.

"Babe? What is it?" He sounded panicked. "Ginny, what happened?"

I took a deep breath and finally found my voice. "Ryan, I can't stay here any longer. I miss my family too much. I love you, but I love them, too. And I can't be without them. I didn't know it was going to be so hard. I'm sorry. I'm so sorry." I sniffed. "I'm going to fly home tonight so I can be there for Christmas." I flopped on the couch and Hershey set her chin on my leg. I scratched her ear.

"Ginny, you just need to—"

"Give it some time. I know, you've told me that so many times. But you're wrong. This feeling isn't going to go away; it's going to get worse."

"It's just the holiday blues."

"No. It's not. Ryan, it's just not going to work. I'm sorry. Please send the rest of my things home. Good luck down here, honey. I know you love it. You'll be fine without me."

"I wish I could come home right now and talk to you, but I can't. Please don't leave."

"There's a storm coming. If I don't leave now, I won't get home in time for Christmas."

"I'm not giving up on you. Go home if you need to, but we're going to talk about this later."

But I had to leave: we weren't engaged, my name wasn't on the mortgage, I had no boss to leave in the lurch. What I did have was a family back home I was missing like crazy. And that thought only resolved my decision.

"I have to go," I whispered," I hung up and bawled. *So this is what it's like to hit bottom.* I'd screwed up everything—for him and for me. If only my cousin Marnie could see me now. I was hardly inspirational.

I fed Hershey and then let her out one last time. I hugged her neck, nuzzling her neck with my nose. "I'll miss you, girl," I said, her fur wet from my tears. She licked my cheek, and leaned into me, like she knew. I took one last look at our little house that had never really felt like a home to me. "Goodbye," I whispered. I waited on the front porch until the cab picked me up to take me to the airport. I didn't have a car anymore. Mine hadn't been reliable enough to make the trip down, so I'd sold it.

Once I got to the airport, I bought a one-way ticket from Tampa to Rochester—which cost a pretty penny so close to the holidays—and thought about calling my parents so they could pick me up when I got in. But I didn't want worry my mother when she had so much to do for the party, and if I heard her voice again, I might break down crying in the terminal. I'd take a cab when I arrived. My flight left at 4:00 p.m. and I'd get in at 7:25. Maybe the girls and I could make decent gingerbread men the next day.

But as I counted down the minutes to my flight, hoping my courage would hold out until we left, an overhead announcement blared out the bad news: my flight was delayed because of the weather. I paced through the concourse, downing more Starbucks than should be legal in one day. My hands were shaking as I tried to read a magazine, and I tried my best to chase away the image of Ryan's smiling face that kept invading my brain. Not so easy—it's a really nice face.

Then my cell rang a little after five. Ryan was home by now. "Hi," I answered quietly. I wasn't sure if he was going to be more sad or mad that I'd actually left

"Ginny, you're really doing this. What happened? Why now?" He sounded hurt; that was even worse.

My throat felt thick and my eyes were filling with tears just at the sound of his voice. I turned away from the man seated next to me reading a newspaper and lowered my voice. "I talked to my mom and my nieces today." My voice was hushed, not only because I was in a public place, but also because the words were so hard to say. "I just didn't realize how much I missed them. And they need me." I sniffed. "But it's more than that. You know when you had to pull over on the highway for me during the move down here? I wasn't just carsick. I was scared I couldn't do this. Turns out, I was right."

The woman sitting across from me hadn't turned

the page of her book in a while. My own personal drama must've been much more interesting than her paperback. I'm sure she wasn't the only one listening, but I couldn't stop now, and I couldn't walk away from my carry-on bags to look for a bit of privacy.

Ryan was quiet for a moment. "Honey, of course you're not happy down here. You don't have a job yet. You haven't had a chance to make friends. You're not yourself. You haven't cracked a joke in weeks. Just give it a few more months."

He was right. My silly sense of humor and good spirits had disappeared. I hadn't baked anything since we'd moved down here, either. Not even chocolate chip cookies. I shook my head, even though he couldn't see me. "It won't. It'd just be putting off the inevitable. I'm going home, and I might as well go now so I don't miss the holidays."

He was quiet for a long while. Apparently, he didn't know what to say either. Finally, he said, "I've got the Weather Channel on. I don't think you're going to be getting in tonight. The storm's worse than they thought."

So is the feeling in my stomach, I thought. And right then an overhead announcement brought me even worse news. "All flights to Rochester, New York are canceled for the rest of the night due to bad weather. Please check with your airline tomorrow morning for rescheduling."

Ryan must have heard it. "Let me come get you."

I couldn't protest; I had nowhere else to go. "Okay. I'll meet you by the baggage claim."

The airline unloaded our luggage, so I grabbed my bags and set it all in a pile by a row of chairs. Sitting down and studying the carpet, I waited for Ryan to show up. A whiff of his aftershave let me know when he'd arrived. I still wouldn't look up, but I didn't resist when he pulled me into his arms. I let myself be hugged. "I'm only coming home for the night. Don't try to talk me out of this."

He kissed my head. "I won't. I want you to stay

more than anything. I love you, babe. But you've got to make the decision that's right for you. We won't be happy unless we both want to be here."

I leaned into him and nodded. He should be yelling at me, but he was being sympathetic and understanding. I was such a jerk. Ryan was a nice guy—and not in a too-bad-he's-not-hot way. He was gorgeous and funny, too—the whole package. He just happened to be living in the wrong place.

I followed him out into the warm night, marveling again at how different it was down here. I was usually shivering and dashing for the car this time of year. Instead, we took our time walking to the parking ramp with my bags, his hand resting on my lower back as I kicked a pebble along.

"Want to go out to eat?" he asked.

I shrugged. I certainly didn't feel like cooking. "Sure. Wherever you want."

He drove me to an Italian restaurant a few blocks from the house. I didn't have much of an appetite, but I knew I should eat or I'd get a headache.

Ryan ordered us wine, and I picked the first thing I saw on the menu—lasagna. Usually a hard dish to screw up. Ryan ordered Fettuccine Alfredo, probably on my account. He knew I loved it, but feared how fattening it was. Stealing a few bites from his plate was always a good consolation.

"So, everyone back home is okay?" he asked, swirling the ice in his drink.

A little laugh escaped. "The girls called me because Mom burned the gingerbread men. We make them every year and decorate them to look like all our family members. They were real upset."

"Then you got upset."

Our salads arrived and I pointed my fork at him. "But it's more than that. I'm going to miss their dance recitals. Game night with my parents. Everything." I closed my eyes and shook my head.

He leaned across the table toward me. "But we have things to look forward to down here. Walks on the beach. Our first crop of oranges from the tree in the backyard. I'm sorry I haven't been around much. It hasn't been fair to you. Things'll calm down after the holidays. I'm covering everyone's vacation time. It won't always be like this."

I looked away. "Stop, please," I whispered, panic swirling in my chest. "I've made up my mind."

He said nothing, but nodded. Then a grin creeped onto his face. "Remember how we met?"

I laughed softly. "Of course. We're probably the only couple to get together at Chuck E. Cheese." I'd been at Brooke's birthday party and he'd been at a party for his friend's son. We'd gotten to know each other over a slice of birthday cake and a handful of game tokens. We'd been together ever since.

"I'm sure you're right. But we didn't expect that, either." He shrugged. "You don't know what's going to happen. Who would've thought we'd be in Florida? Life's an adventure, and I want you with me to experience it all, Ginny."

I pushed a cherry tomato around on my plate. "I want to be with you, too. But not down here."

He looked at me and sighed, then nodded like he understood.

We finished dinner in silence, not filled with anger, but resignation. I was no longer wishing I were in the midst of the snowstorm anymore; I wanted the damn thing to be over so I could get home.

After dinner, Ryan walked me to his car and paused before he opened my door for me. He said nothing, just took me in his arms and kissed my head. "Why don't you go home for the holidays for a few days? A visit will do you good. Maybe you're just homesick. I'd come with you, but I can't get any time off."

I exhaled. I was pretty sure if I went home for a visit, I wouldn't want to come back. "A visit's not enough."

We drove home and he dropped me off at the house, explaining he was going to the grocery store. "We're out of ice cream, and I want to get a few things before the stores get crowded tomorrow."

I nodded, wondering if he was just being thoughtful and giving me my space. That's the kind of sweet thing Ryan was always doing. After he left, I checked online to see if flights had been rescheduled yet, but so far, everything still said canceled.

I clicked on the live weather cam from the local TV station in Rochester. I could see nothing more than the hulking images of cars lining a city street, covered in mounds of snow. The picture was a near whiteout. I clicked off the site. My heart had swelled seeing Ryan at the airport. But he hadn't changed my mind; I was going home the next day. For good.

Two hours had passed and Ryan still wasn't home. I wondered if he'd gone out for a drink. I couldn't blame him. I turned the air conditioning down a notch, crawled under the covers, and imagined myself home in bed under my down comforter. I tried to ignore the tug at my heart, realizing Ryan wouldn't be there with me. Tears spilled down my cheeks and I cried myself to sleep.

***

I woke the next morning to find Ryan shaking my arm. I didn't even know if he'd come to bed or slept on the couch—or if he was just coming in from a night out. "Honey, get up. You're not going to believe this."

I rubbed my eyes and propped myself on my elbow. "Is it about my flight?"

He grinned, his gorgeous dimples showing up in his cheeks. "Let's just say I don't think you're going to get out today."

My stomach fell. I didn't know if I could take another day stuck here, convincing myself that going home was a good idea. Not with Ryan and his sexy gray eyes, his strong arms that felt so good around me, and his sweet, kind voice telling me all the right things. But if I didn't leave, I was sure we'd be going through this exact same scenario a few months down the road.

I sat up and blinked at him. "Why are you wearing a scarf and hat?"

"Come and see for yourself." He took me by the hand and led me to the family room. Then he threw open the curtains. "We're snowed in!"

I squinted at the windows, covered in white. "Are you kidding me? In Florida?" I walked closer and ran my finger across the pane, leaving a streak in the fuzzy white covering; it was fake snow from a can. I looked around our little house and noticed they were all like that. I strapped my arms across my chest, trying to suppress my grin. "What're you doing?"

He stuck his head out the door and quickly closed it. He pretended to shiver. "It's horrible out. We might be stuck inside all day. Luckily, I made some hot chocolate." He pointed to the coffee table and two steaming mugs, with marshmallows bobbing on top.

The lump in my throat left me speechless. This was totally unexpected. Much like the way we'd met.

"It's the perfect snowy day to decorate our tree," he said. A real Christmas tree was now mounted in the stand, and Ryan had pulled out the rest of our ornaments. He flicked on some Christmas carols. The familiar sounds of the Nutcracker Suite filled the room.

I closed my eyes and inhaled the scent of pine. My throat was tight and the words couldn't find my lips. I dropped my head in my hands and started to cry.

He rushed next to me and squeezed my shoulder. "I'm sorry, honey. Don't cry. I thought you'd like this." He rubbed my back and I leaned against him, unable to say anything. How could I explain all the emotions swirling inside me? The sadness over moving from home, the fear of this strange new place, and maybe even fear over the commitment of moving in together. Did I really want to leave him?

"I know it's not New York, but we can pretend it's just like home."

I sniffed and nodded. "I like it. I really do."

A relieved smile appeared. "Wanna hit the beach and make a sandman?"

I gave him a funny look, but broke out in giggles. "Are you sure we can get to the beach with all this snow?"

He readjusted his scarf. "We'll give it try."

We brought our hot chocolate along, and he pulled me outside. Big plastic candy canes lined our sidewalk. An inflatable Santa in a sled sat perched in front of the house. The gutters were lined with white icicle lights. I turned to him. "Did you stay up all night doing this?"

He shrugged. "Pretty much. After the grocery store, I hit Save Land. I was the last customer out."

Edna came out of her front door and came into our yard. "Finally, some decorations. Looks great!" She handed me a package wrapped in tinfoil with a red bow on top. "Merry Christmas! They still talk about my fruitcake back in Michigan, you know."

"Thanks so much! I should've made some cookies, but I've been…"

She waved her hand. "You've been busy settling in. It's not always easy, you know. But next year I'll be looking for some cookies from you." She winked at me, and went back to her house.

I handed the fruitcake to Ryan. "You carry this—it's heavy."

We made the quick ride to the beach. Grabbing our mugs, the fruitcake, and a blanket, we settled on the sand.

"This is a first. Drinking hot chocolate on the beach."

He put his arm around me. "There's a lot of firsts for us here, Ginny. I promise to make more time for you. And next time you get homesick, I'll make sure to really listen." He kissed my hand and I leaned into him. He really wanted me to stay.

We opened the fruitcake, took a quick sample, and decided it would make a nice treat for the seagulls. They swooped around us as we tossed bits and pieces up into the air. Ryan and I laughed as the birds squawked at each other and fought over the crumbs.

"Now what about that sandman?" Ryan asked. He balled up a mound of sand, making it bigger and bigger, then tried to add a second tier. Our hands and legs were dirty and sandy, but we giggled with each attempt as clumps of sand spilled to the ground.

Finally we decided you couldn't make a snowman out of sand. Ryan shrugged. "We tried."

"But there are other fun things to do at the beach." I grabbed a handful of sand and threw it at Ryan.

He ducked out of the way. "What was that for?" he asked, as the spray of sand flew past him.

"It's a Florida snowball. Or it was supposed to be." I scooped up another handful and tossed it at him again.

Pretending to be hit, Ryan fell back on the ground. Then he swooshed his arms and legs in the sand, leaving the imprint of an angel. This buff, six-foot-two guy was acting like a total kid, and it only made me crazier about him.

"You need to work on your technique. Learn from a pro." I flopped down next to him and made one of my own. Ryan rolled over next to me and took me in his arms, kissing me gently. "Couldn't do this at home, kissing outside like this. We'd be freezing our tails off."

I sighed as he held me. "That's true."

"And I see a lot more of your gorgeous body down here, now that it's not all covered up in sweaters and coats." He kissed me again. "And that makes me want to do more of this." He slid his hand up under my shirt, trailing his fingertips along my spine.

I shivered. "So there are a few benefits, I guess."

95

Aware that the few people on the beach were starting to stare, I whispered, "Let's go home." *Home*, I said to myself again. Could this really be my home?

We held hands on the ride back. "I've got an early present for you," he said.

"Now you're talking my language."

We went inside and he reached for a pastry box on top of the refrigerator and handed it to me. Our fingers brushed, and I got another rush of shivers; he still had that effect on me.

"What is this?" I pulled the red ribbon off the box. Inside, was a gingerbread woman, with long strands of yellow frosting piped along her face for the hair. She also sported a red bikini, just like mine, and a Santa hat. I looked up at Ryan. "That's me!" Next to my cookie was one that looked like Ryan.

He nodded. "They're probably not as good as the ones you make, but I knew they were important to you. And the bakery had a sign in the window that they were looking for a pastry chef." He raised one eyebrow.

"Really?" My heart raced at the idea. I felt a glimmer of excitement I hadn't felt since we'd left Rochester.

He nodded, then checked his watch. "Do you want to check your flight status?"

Was I really going to leave this funny, charming man? He hadn't done anything wrong. He hadn't insisted I move here with him. I came because I wanted to be with him. And I was bailing the moment it got difficult? What kind of girlfriend was I? I didn't deserve him. I shook my head. "Not now."

He nodded and smiled. "Good. I thought we could go out pick out some new ornaments later, something to remind us of our new life down here," he said. "Our new adventure together."

"You're something else." And he was. I could find a home anywhere; a wonderful man like Ryan was irreplaceable. How had I been so stupid not to realize it?

Here I'd threatened to leave him, and he'd been patient and understanding. Most guys would've blown a gasket. Men like Ryan didn't come around often.

Ryan grabbed my hand and brought me to the tree. We hung the ornaments we did have and tossed tinsel at each other. We ended up on the floor laughing, then kissing—like one of those crazy-in-love kisses when you first start dating.

Then he planted a smooch on my forehead. "I know you gave up a lot to come with me. But it doesn't matter where we are, as long as we're together," he said, holding me.

I closed my eyes and snuggled against him. "You're right. *You're* my home, wherever we are. And we need to start some new traditions here."

"Like our annual Florida blizzard?" he asked.

"Exactly. Now help me get that Christmas village out and then we'll make cookies." I stood up and held out my hand to pull him up.

"More gingerbread men?"

I stopped and thought. "No, this year we'll try something new. Cut-outs with a little orange flavoring. In honor of our new beginning and all." Something to show we really were home now. Something I'd miss if we happened to move again.

I knew then that I'd follow Ryan anywhere. My angst and longing for home disappeared. And that was a wonderful gift for us both.

"I really want you to stay, but what about that plane ticket? I understand if you still want to go home for the holidays. I'll drive you to the airport when the weather clears. You could get there in time for Christmas and come back in a few days."

I shook my head. "I wouldn't want to miss our first Christmas together. I'll save my trip home for after the holidays."

His smile hit me square in the heart. "You sure?"

I couldn't hold back my grin. "I finally realized I'm

97

right where I want to be—with you."

His eyes twinkled like jolly old St. Nick himself—minus the beard and belly. "In that case, maybe I can give you one more Christmas present early."

I raised an eyebrow. "Even better than the cookies?"

"Just a little bit." He got down on one knee and grabbed my hands in his. "Ginny, I should have made this commitment before I brought you down here. But with the cost of the house and moving, I had to wait to get this. Luckily, I've been putting in some overtime." He winked and then pulled a sparkling ring from his pocket. "Will you marry me?"

I dropped to my knees beside him and wrapped my arms around him. "Yes," I finally managed to say. I sobbed in his arms for a few minutes and stared at the ring on my finger to convince myself it was actually there. I wiggled my fingers to make it sparkle in the light.

"Do you like it? I was going to save it until Christmas, but this seemed like a good time."

"I love it." The words came out in a whisper and I cleared my throat. "Do you want your Christmas present now?" I asked. New running gear would pale in comparison, but still.

He grinned, and scooped me up in his arms. "I've got what I want right here."

I cocked an eyebrow at him. "Then take your present to the bedroom and unwrap it, fool."

"Now there's the Ginny I remember. Guess I can shovel the driveway later."

I playfully whacked him as he carried me down the hall to our future.

"Tingle All The Way"
by Lisa Scott

By the time Jessica finished watching *Love, Actually,* and cleaned up the popcorn bowl and hot chocolate, it was 11:50 on Christmas Eve. She looked at the hands on the clock nearing midnight. "Big whoop, it's almost Christmas," she said to her cat snoozing on the couch. Snickers opened one eye and rolled over.

Unfortunately, the movie had done nothing to put her in the holiday mood. Not even the big snowstorm that had covered Rochester in a blanket of white had gotten her in the proper spirit. Nothing could.

The holidays weren't her thing. She wasn't like her sister, Lindy, who tossed imaginary glitter and sparkles wherever she went during the holidays, convinced every Christmas could be a magical, marvelous miracle in the making. *Blech.* And this year had been a magnificent holiday for Lindy. She'd landed a new job and a great guy, while Jessica still watched sappy movies all by herself without shedding a tear. That's how much of an icicle queen she was.

It didn't help that she lived in her childhood home, and her disappointing Christmas memories could be relived by staring into the living room. She didn't necessarily dislike the holidays; she was just immune to them. Kind of like being colorblind, she supposed. Who knew what blue really looked like if you'd never seen it? Well, she'd never felt the giddiness so many people experienced this time of year. She was holiday blind. Yeah, that was it.

She hadn't bothered with a Christmas tree. And mistletoe? What's the use? There'd be no impromptu kissing here. You couldn't really do that without a guy around and it had been a while since one had come calling.

She checked the lock on the front door and

flicked off the lights but then something caught her eye outside. Was someone breaking into her neighbor's house?

She knelt in front of the living room window, resting her chin on the sill. Her quick breaths left puffs of steam on the glass; the pane was cold against her nose.

She squinted at the figure climbing a ladder propped up against the house. It was a man, Jessica was sure of it. She knew her neighbor Sally didn't have a boyfriend, and her husband had left her a few months ago. So who was this guy? Sally's car wasn't in the driveway, but someone else's was. Her heart quickened.

She wasn't going to watch her neighbor get robbed blind. She dashed for the phone and called 911.

"911 what's your emergency?"

"Someone's breaking into my neighbor's house. Looks like a guy on a ladder is trying to crawl through a window. Hurry!"

Jessica gave them the address and decided to put on some clothes Surely, they'd want a statement from the woman who'd stopped a holiday robbery, and Jessica didn't want to be doing that while wearing thermal pajamas covered with sledding penguins. What if they took her picture for the paper? She could just imagine the headline: "Local Woman Saves Christmas." If her sister had gotten on the news for locking herself in a Save Land dressing room, then she'd definitely make headlines for this. She smiled to herself as she hurried to her closet. Who said she couldn't find the Christmas spirit?

***

Charlie slid the skis through the window as he wobbled on the ladder. *Don't let me fall now.* He'd almost completed his mission, and toppling off the ladder would ruin everything. Sirens split the night and he hoped they wouldn't wake Morgan before he got inside. He had to make this the perfect Christmas. It'd been a tough year for the little girl.

He looked behind him, pleased with his work. It

had taken a while to figure it all out, but walking backward on hooves he'd fashioned out of hunks of wood tacked on top of tiny stilts had certainly left the impression that a herd of reindeer had landed in the yard. Sliding the skis through the snow made it appear as if Santa's sleigh had touched down. Then he'd walked back through the tracks to the ladder, where he was trying slip back inside through the window. *Uncle of the Year*, he congratulated himself.

Two cop cars pulled up in front of the house. Car doors flew open, and one of the cops yelled, "Freeze! Show your hands!"

Shit. He raised his hands and tried to look behind him, but the ladder teetered and he reached to grab the gutter above him. But he missed, and landed in the snow—the ladder clattering down on over him.

Right on top of the reindeer prints that had taken an hour to perfect.

The cops ran to him, guns held high, and Charlie stuck his hands up. His face was stuck between two rungs. If not for the heavy snow pack, he'd be in a world of pain.

"Who are you and what are you doing?"

His heart hammered in his chest. "My sister and niece live here. I was leaving hoof prints outside. I was trying to climb back through the window so I that I didn't leave footprints on the lawn." He winced, thinking of all *their* footprints all over the lawn.

One of the cops was kind enough to pull the ladder off him. "Do you have ID on you?"

"In the house."

"Let's go get it."

***

Jessica cupped her face as she peered out the window, waiting for the press to show up. That's when she'd run outside and give them the scoop. She did a double-take. *Wait a minute … they're going inside with him? What the hell?*

Throwing on a coat and boots, she ran out the

door. One of the cops was waiting by the cruiser, so she approached him. "Hi, I'm the one who called 911. Did you catch him? Was he robbing the place?" She was breathless.

The officer shrugged. "The officers are trying to figure that out right now."

With that, the two cops followed the suspect out of the house, one of them shaking his hand. "We're really sorry, sir."

Why aren't they arresting him?

The guy ran his hands through his hair. "I understand. But who called the police?"

"That would be this woman here," the officer next to Jessica said.

Flustered, she put her hands on her hips. "Why were you crawling through the window? And who are you? I know Sally and she doesn't have any guys in her life right now."

He walked toward her and stopped about a foot away, crossing his arms. She hadn't realized he was cute when she'd thought he was a robber. "I'm Charlie Grant, Sally's brother. She has to work late at the airport getting all those cancelled flights in, so I'm watching Morgan. Since she's going to wake up to no Mommy, I thought I'd try to make it an extra special Christmas for her with hoof prints in the yard." He stomped his feet in the snow and mumbled, "I kind of promised her she'd be able to see proof Santa had been here. She's lost a bit of the holiday spirit."

Jessica gulped and her stomach tumbled. "But the ladder?"

He gestured behind him. "Climbing in and out of the window was the only way to avoid leaving my footprints back to the front door. That would be a little obvious to a seven-year-old."

Just then a car pulled up and a photographer jumped out with a camera. He approached one of the officers. "Hey, Chris Henry from the paper. What's going on here? A Christmas robbery?"

The cop rubbed his chin. "Not exactly. This guy here was trying to create some magical Christmas scene outside for his niece. But his neighbor called 911 when she saw him climbing through the window."

"The magic's kind of gone now," Charlie said staring at the yard.

The photographer snapped a picture of them lamenting over the trampled front yard.

"So, who was the Grinch that called this in?" the photographer asked with a chuckle.

Jessica wagged a finger at him. "Hey, I'm not a Grinch. I thought I was thwarting a robbery." That was a nice big word for the paper—thwarting. She pointed at Charlie. "He doesn't live here. I thought he was a stranger."

Charlie set his hand on her arm. "It's okay. I appreciate you looking out for my sister and niece. It's just been a rough year for her, and I wanted this Christmas to be really special for Morgan; get her mind off all the tough stuff."

And with that, a curly-haired girl rubbing her eyes wandered onto the front porch.

"Oh, crap," Charlie mumbled. He ran toward her. "Morgan, you should be in bed, or Santa won't come."

"I think he did come, but he didn't wrap all my presents." She pointed to the unwrapped boxes and gifts scattered by the door on the living room floor, and the rolls of wrapping paper.

Charlie scratched his head. "Uh, maybe he got scared off when he heard the police sirens."

Morgan stuck out her lower lip and pouted. "Why are the police here? Is Santa in trouble?"

The cops looked at each other and Jessica stared at the ground covered in fresh footprints. She faced the little girl. "It was my fault, sweetie. It's me, Jessica from across the street." She pointed to her house.

Morgan stared at her, gripping a grungy stuffed animal under her arm.

Charlie turned to Jessica with an expectant look on his face.

Taking a deep breath, Jessica tried to channel her creative-lying gene. It was in there somewhere; she'd used it extensively throughout high school. "I heard something outside." She pin-wheeled her arms, as if that might generate the rest of the tale.

"You probably heard Santa," Morgan said.

"No, it didn't sound jolly or like a reindeer…" She twisted her lips, trying to remember what noise reindeer made. "I didn't hear any neighing."

Morgan shook her head. "Reindeer don't make noise. Their bells jingle, that's all. You called police because of jingle bells?"

Jessica crossed her arms. "No, no. This wasn't jingling. It was scary, like a monster."

Morgan's eyes widened and Charlie rolled his.

"No, no, no. It wasn't like a monster, it was like…"

Morgan interrupted her. "It *was* Santa, and you scared him away before he could leave all my presents and he's not going to come back." She stomped her foot and stormed back inside, slamming the door behind her. Charlie chased after her.

"Nicely done," the photographer said, snapping another shot of her. "It's not as juicy as a Christmas hold-up, but this'll make a nice fluff piece—Nosy Neighbor Mars Magic of Christmas."

Her jaw dropped, but it was hard to protest the truth.

Mumbling to each other, the cops headed for their cruisers.

Well, good grief. Her Christmas funk was contagious. Maybe she should hunker down until after New Year's.

Too bad she hadn't stocked up on chocolate and

wine.

***

Once she collapsed into bed, she stared at the ceiling. No visions of sugarplums danced in *her* head. Instead, she was haunted by Morgan's sad face. Was Morgan going to give up on the magic of Christmas the same way that she had?

Of course, giving up wasn't exactly right. She'd never bought into the joy of the holiday. She couldn't remember that wonderful Christmas Lindy referred to so often. Jessica was only a year and a half old when their mother died. While Lindy was relishing the boatload of presents she'd gotten from Santa—which Lindy figured had been some sort of consolation prize since they'd lost their mother—Jessica had probably been chewing on her fist. Their father had always been sullen around Christmas as far as Jessica could remember. Lindy was the one who lived for the holiday.

She thought about the disappointment in Morgan's eyes. A shot of pain clamped around her heart. *I ruined Christmas for that little girl.* She sat up in bed. "I'm going to make it up to her. Tomorrow, I'm going to give Morgan the best Christmas she's ever had."

She snuggled up against her pillow and smiled, thinking of all the wonderful holiday things they could do together the next day. Knowing Morgan's hottie uncle would be there made her smile even more.

As long as she could forget that he probably hated her right now.

***

Once he was certain Morgan was asleep—it'd taken a good twenty minutes before she'd conked out—Charlie started wrapping the rest of her gifts. He had no idea how to salvage the holiday, now. He certainly wasn't going to call Sally and give her the bad news. She felt guilty enough as it was missing Christmas morning with her daughter. But money talks; especially for a single mother offered triple time. He didn't blame her. He just

105

hoped Morgan didn't either.

He clenched his teeth, thinking how close he'd come to pulling this off. If only that neighbor had minded her own business. But he felt guilty being angry, because she did have good intentions. And he couldn't help but chuckle remembering her bemused face when she'd learned the truth.

He flicked off the lights on the Christmas tree and shuffled off to bed. He had no idea how he was going to make it up to Morgan the next day. They'd gone to church earlier that night. His mom was having a party for the family on Christmas night, and Sally wouldn't be home until two o'clock in the afternoon.

What was he going to do with a disappointed seven-year-old during all that time?

***

Disappointed or not, Morgan was up at 8:00 a.m., raring to go. "Uncle Charlie, let's open presents!"

Rubbing his eyes, he followed her out to the Christmas tree. She gazed at all the presents, then put her hands on her hips and leveled him with a stare. "You finished wrapping the presents, didn't you?"

He thought about lying, but then said, "I did. I wasn't sure if Santa had time to come back or not. How did you know?"

"They're really messy. Santa's presents always look very pretty."

He laughed. He'd been in a hurry, what could he say?

She shrugged and found a spot to sit in front of the tree. He snapped a few photos, and then let her attack the presents.

Paper and bows flew through the air as she unwrapped art supplies and stuffed animals. Morgan squealed when she peeled the wrapping off some giant plastic contraption with little animals. At least putting that together would keep him busy for a while.

When it was all over, the place looked like the

scene of a home invasion. If the cops had shown up now, they'd surely think he'd robbed the place. He sighed, remembering how thrilled he'd been with his setup outside—until it had become a potential crime scene.

"When's Mommy coming home?" Morgan asked. "I miss her."

He gathered her on his lap. "Later today. She's helping people get home to their families for Christmas."

"I wish she could get home to our family." She sniffed. "How come Daddy didn't send me any presents?"

"You're going to see Daddy in a few weeks when he comes home. He'll have your presents then. Remember, he told you on the phone yesterday?"

She stuck her thumb in her mouth and leaned against him. Sally had been so worried about this regression in Morgan. She hadn't sucked her thumb since she was three. But her doctor said it was normal for kids going through trauma.

Trauma. He winced at the word. Then he squeezed her arm. "Why don't I get your animal thing set up and you can start working on some of those crafts?"

"Okay. But I'm hungry. Mommy always makes a special Christmas breakfast. Are you going to make it?"

He stifled a groan. Sally hadn't told him about that. "What does she make?"

Morgan shrugged. "A breakfast pie."

What? Charlie was lucky to pull off toast that wasn't burnt, or cereal that had the right balance of flakes to milk. "Maybe she can make that tomorrow. Let's see what we've got in the kitchen."

While Morgan went back to examine her presents, Charlie inspected the contents of the fridge. Talk about the cupboard being bare. He rifled through the cabinets and found some Pop tarts, marshmallows, and peanut butter. Kids liked that stuff, right?

He piled the selections on a plate and brought it

out to Morgan. She looked up at him, alarmed. "What's this?"

"Stuff. Fun stuff."

Morgan crossed her arms. "Not for Christmas breakfast."

"Want cereal—without milk?"

Tears spilled out of her eyes. This was going to be a long day.

***

Jessica was waiting in front of Save Land when the doors finally opened at nine. Her sister put the store keys in her pocket and blinked at her. "What's going on?"

Jessica pushed past Lindy and grabbed a cart. "I ruined a little girl's Christmas last night and I'm trying to make it right."

"Oh, so you're acknowledging that it's Christmas today. I thought maybe you weren't recognizing it this year."

Jessica rolled her eyes.

Lindy's gorgeous new boyfriend, the store manager, came up behind Lindy and hugged her. She recognized him from his TV interview when Lindy had gotten locked in the store overnight.

"This is my sister, Jessica," Lindy said.

"Nice to meet you and Merry Christmas."

"Same to you." Jessica shook his hand. "I was just telling my sister I need some major holiday mojo this year. Last minute of course. Thank God you're open." She cocked her head. "Do you guys sell Mrs. Clause outfits here?" Maybe that would get everyone in the spirit.

Alex pinched the bridge of his nose. "No, but I promise, we will next year."

"Alex and I are going out to dinner tonight. Want to join us?" Lindy asked.

"Probably not." Jessica hurried back to the toy department and froze as she eyed the aisles and aisles of toys. She had no idea what seven-year-old girls liked these days. She tried thinking back to when she was seven, but couldn't remember much beyond coloring books and crayons. *Did kids even do that today?*

She turned down an aisle and stared at the rows of Barbies and Barbie-look-alikes. *Every girl likes those*, she thought. She didn't know if she could make it up to Morgan with gifts, but Lindy had never forgotten that bountiful Christmas so long ago, so maybe it'd be the same for Morgan.

Jessica tossed three different dolls in the cart along with outfits, and a Barbie dollhouse that cost an astonishing amount of money, but would be worth it. She grabbed crayons and coloring books—just in case—and snagged a roll of wrapping paper. There wasn't much left and she wasn't thrilled with the polar-bears-conducting-trains design, but what else could she do?

She wheeled her cart to the register and, of course, Lindy was manning it. "Seriously?" she asked.

Jessica crossed her arms. "Let's just call it major damage control." Her eyes popped when Lindy announced the total—even after Lindy applied her employee discount.

"Hope this helps, kiddo," she said.

Jessica gulped. "Me, too. You two have fun tonight."

"We will." Lindy giggled that newly-in-love giggle that sounded like unmanicured fingernails on a chalkboard to Jessica. But her big sister deserved to be happy.

"Merry Christmas, Lindy."

Lindy hurried around to hug her. "You, too. You never know, it could be a Christmas to remember."

She forced a grin. "I am one-hundred percent positive this is going to be a Christmas to forget." *I only hope I'll be able to*, she thought as she dashed to the car with her bags.

When she got home, she quickly wrapped the gifts, then double-checked her hair and makeup. As if

Charlie would give her second look after she imploded their Christmas. But she didn't need to worsen the situation by scaring Morgan with dark circles and eye baggage.

Taking a deep breath, she put on her coat and carried the gifts across the street. She rang the doorbell and stepped back, resting her chin on top of the Barbie house and holding the rest of the gifts in a bag. She hoped the door wouldn't be slammed in her face.

The door opened and she sucked in a shock of cold air. Somehow, Charlie looked even more handsome without the red glare of the police lights, especially with his stubbled chin and tousled hair. He looked entirely adorable in his flannel pajama bottoms and long-sleeved red shirt. With a reindeer on front of it—the perfect snuggle-on-the-couch outfit.

She shifted from one foot to another. "Hi," she said. "It's me. From across the street." Her insides hummed despite her nervousness. She couldn't remember the last time she'd felt like this just looking a guy.

He forced a grin and nodded. "I remember."

She cleared her throat. "Well, it looks like Santa left some of Morgan's presents at my house. Can I come in?"

He looked at the presents and then into her eyes, a bit uncertain. "Sure." He gestured for her to come inside, then reached out and grabbed the newspaper that had been delivered on the front porch. He tossed it on a bench in the front hall, and she spotted the headline at the bottom of the page, "Nosy Neighbor Mars Magic of Christmas."

He must have seen her wince, because he flipped the paper over so the headline was no longer visible. "I thought he was joking about that."

She groaned. "I wish. But my Christmas wishes usually don't come true."

Morgan scampered over to the front hall. She

crossed her arms and glared, probably replaying the scene from the night before in her head. "Jessica? Why are you here?"

Jessica set the pile of presents on the hall bench. "I woke up and found all these presents from Santa at my house addressed to you."

Her eyes widened. "Really?" she whispered.

Jessica nodded. "Santa must have gotten confused last night with all that police business. Why don't you open them?"

Morgan hopped around and squealed while Charlie carried them into the living room and set them in front of the tree. "Go for it, kiddo."

Jessica clapped. "Isn't this the best Christmas ever? Bonus presents! That hardly ever happens. I never got a present as big as that one when I was little. Never. And I always wished for a huge, big surprise present." She shrugged. "Never got one. But you did. Open it!" Gosh, she sounded like one of Santa's helpers. How was she pulling this off? She sat down on the couch to enjoy the show.

"I know! I'm so lucky. This is awesome! I'm going to open the small one first. Then the big one." Morgan's face glowed with excitement and she tore open the giant box of crayons and the coloring books. Then her smile faded. "Crayons? I don't remember asking for crayons. I wonder why Santa brought them?"

Charlie cleared his throat. "Santa must know how much you like doing art projects."

"Right. But I use pastels and colored pencils, now. I haven't used crayons since I was three."

Jessica's heart fell, but she kept her grin in place. "Maybe he thought you should give them another try."

Charlie gave Jessica an apologetic smile. He turned to Morgan. "Open the rest of them."

"I can't wait to see what's in the big one!" She looked more closely at the paper, made a funny face, then shrugged and ripped off the wrapping. She scrunched up

111

her nose and looked at Charlie. "A Barbie house? I don't even like Barbies. Santa knows that. I told him so at the mall." She cocked her head and looked at Jessica. "Are you sure these were supposed to be for me?"

Her throat was tight as she faked a smile. "That's what the tags said. Maybe Santa confused your list with someone else's?" She shrugged and tried to sound breezy.

Morgan quietly opened the rest of the gifts; all those Barbies she didn't like. She sighed when she was done and wandered over to Charlie, leaving the toys strewn about the floor. "Can we call Mommy?"

Charlie rubbed her back. "She told me she'd call when she got a break."

Morgan nodded. "What are we going to do until then?"

Jessica felt like running back home and crawling under her covers. For a week. But no, she refused to give up that easily. She stood and held up a finger. "We are going to make Christmas cookies."

Charlie grinned at her. "Good luck with that. There's not much in the fridge."

She reached for her coat. "Then I'll go raid my kitchen and be right back." Tears filled her eyes as she trudged across the street. Only she could show up with gifts and make a child's rotten holiday worse.

Raiding her kitchen, she filled a grocery bag with flour, sugar, butter, milk and the decorating items she'd need to make cut-outs. That was bound to be fun and they could take their time decorating them. That ought to please the little artist pouting over crayons. Jessica had made cut-out cookies once years ago, but grabbed her recipe book in case she'd forgotten how.

***

As Charlie balled up the wrapping paper, he kept his lecture on being grateful short. He got eye rolls from Morgan anyway. The phone rang and Morgan dashed to answer it. "Hi, Mommy!" she said, even before asking who it was.

Though it must have been Sally after all, because Morgan rambled off the list of presents she'd received, explained about the police, and then Jessica's visit. She held the phone out. "Mommy wants to talk to you!"

I'm sure she does. Charlie grabbed the phone. "Merry Christmas, sis."

"I work one measly holiday and all hell breaks loose. What happened?"

"I'll explain it all later. Her dad called and talked to her last night, but she's still feeling down. When are you coming home?"

"Two o'clock. Then I'm going to rest a while before we go to Mom's."

"So, Jessica seems nice," he said, rubbing the back of his head.

"Is my little brother interested in somebody finally?"

"No, no. I'm not." He never could lie to his sister very well. "I just mean she's pretty. And funny. Unintentionally, anyway."

"I don't know her that well. I'm surprised she's going to such lengths for Morgan."

"She feels really bad about last night."

"It's good to know she was looking out for me. Hang in there, I'll be home soon."

When he hung up, the doorbell rang. It was Jessica again, holding an armful of baking supplies. "Who's ready to bake up some holiday fun?" Her cheery attitude seemed forced, as did her smile. He had to fight back his own grin.

Morgan followed her to the kitchen table. "I love cookies. What kind are we going to make?"

"Cut-outs. Can you get me a mixing bowl and some measuring cups?"

Morgan nodded and hurried to the cupboards.

Jessica turned to Charlie. "Do you know how to work the stove?"

Holding up both hands, he took a step back. "I

could barely manage cereal this morning."

She rolled her eyes, but laughed. "I'll figure it out." She inspected the buttons and knobs on the stove, and managed to turn it on.

"Can I help?" he asked.

"Of course." This time her smile seemed real. She laid out the ingredients, and he scrounged around for cookie sheets.

"Do you make a lot of Christmas cookies?" Morgan asked, leaning against the table.

"Nope. I haven't made cookies for a few years. Luckily, my sister forced a cookie cutter set on me one holiday, so I've got everything we need. She's just kind of crazy about Christmas."

Charlie raised an eyebrow. "But you're not?"

She sighed as she measured out a cup of flour and handed it to Morgan to pour into the bowl. "I've never had a great Christmas. My mom died when I was little, and Lindy talks about this magical Christmas, with tons of presents and happiness, but I was too little to remember. After that, most holidays were pretty gloomy. My dad usually lapsed into a funk around the holidays, but Lindy remained ever-hopeful for another fantastic Christmas." She dumped a cup of sugar into the bowl. "Can you go get a great big spoon?" she asked Morgan.

Morgan nodded and skipped over to the silverware drawer, rummaging through the contents.

Charlie lowered his voice. "I appreciate what you're doing."

Jessica gave a little smile but wouldn't look at him. "I hate the thought of being the reason a child had a sad Christmas. I wish when I was a kid, someone would have done something for me like you tried to do last night." Finally, she looked up at him, and laid her hand across her heart. "I'm so sorry I ruined it. I really am."

He squeezed her arm, and was surprised by the effect the move had on him. "You didn't mean to do it."

Morgan ran back to them brandishing a big spoon.

"Here, I found one."

Jessica stared at him with her beautiful blue eyes and he pulled his hand away.

She blushed and looked down. "Thanks, Morgan. Now stir up everything in the bowl."

While Morgan did that, Jessica creamed butter and eggs with a splash of vanilla. "For a non-cookie baker, it looks like you know what you're doing," he said.

She shrugged. "Guess it's like riding a bike."

Soon, they were pressing metal cookie cutters into the pale dough, peeling off snowmen, ornaments, and stars from the table. They filled up two trays and slid them into the oven. Jessica set the timer for ten minutes. "We'll let them cool off before we frost them."

Morgan squealed. "I can't wait!" Charlie was relieved her mood had improved.

Jessica made frosting while Morgan inspected the decorations she was going to use. "These are going to be the best cookies ever! I can't wait to show Mommy. But I want to eat one before she gets home. Is that okay?"

"Of course!" he said.

The timer buzzed and Jessica grabbed two potholders from the counter. When she opened the oven, smoke wafted out. She stepped back, coughing, then grabbed the sheets of cookies. Her face fell. "They're burnt! They were only in there for ten minutes! Her oven must bake hotter than what the temperature reads."

Morgan's lip wobbled and she ran from the room.

"We can make more!" Charlie called after her.

Jessica shook her head. "I don't have any more butter. Think there's any in the fridge?"

"No. I should've gone grocery shopping for them last night."

Jessica slumped into a chair. "I'm just making this day worse and worse for her."

He sat next to her and set his hand on her shoulder. "It's the thought that counts."

"Not when you're a kid!" She sniffed. "This has got to be the worst Christmas ever."

His ex always said he didn't know how to comfort a woman. She'd said it so often he'd just always tuned her out. But now he realized there might have been a grain of truth in that particular accusation. Uninspired in bed? Nah. She'd been wrong about that. But lack of comforting skills or not, he couldn't let Jessica blame herself for a botched holiday.

"I'm sure someone somewhere is having a worse Christmas. Like, anyone in prison," he offered.

She looked at him and tears pooled in her eyes.

Shit. He reached for her hand. "We can fix this."

She shook her head and gathered the rest of her supplies. "I'll just make it worse." She snatched her cookbook off the table. "I'm out of ideas on how to make this up to her. I know you really wanted to make some special memories this morning. I'm sorry I screwed it all up."

"Stay. We can watch a movie or something."

She shook her head. "I have to go."

Oh, of course. How stupid of him. Had he figured she'd stay here all day? That would've been fine with him. But she probably had plans with her family. "Okay. I hope the rest of your Christmas is great, Jessica." *And I hope to see you again.*

She gave him a weak smile. "You, too."

He closed the door behind her wishing his ex hadn't been right—he knew nothing about consoling a woman. The sobs coming from the family room reminded him there was a smaller, younger woman waiting to be disappointed by him, too. He went to find her, wondering if there was any way to make this right for Morgan.

And for Jessica.

***

Jessica dumped her ingredients on the counter and searched the cupboards chocolate. Nothing. And she was out of ice cream, too. Too bad she'd left the icing with Charlie and Morgan. She could've eaten it by the spoonful, that's how lousy she was feeling.

Her cell rang and she saw her sister's ID pop up. Lindy would just keep calling, so Jessica answered.

"How'd Project Santa go?" she asked. "Isn't it fun making Christmas dreams come true? You should have done this years ago."

Jessica laughed into the phone to mask her tears. "She hated the gifts I brought and I burned the cookies we were going to decorate."

Lindy was silent. "Oh, honey. I'm so sorry. Please come out with us tonight. I can't stand the thought of you alone and sad on Christmas."

Yes, nothing like hanging out with two perfectly-happy love birds to cheer up a depressed, lonely girl. "That's okay. It's just another day. Really. I'm fine. Have fun. We'll talk later this week."

"At least let me drop off your presents today."

Jessica sighed. "If you must."

"You know I must. I'll stop by after work."

Jessica hung up and found a bag of chocolate chips. She quickly downed a handful, but didn't feel any better.

She puttered around the house, catching up on cleaning. It was either that or curl up in bed and wait for Christmas to be over. After she finished vacuuming, she stared out the front window at the house across the street. Sally's car was in the driveway, and Charlie's was still there, too. By now, Sally must've heard the whole story. Jessica really wanted to apologize. And yes, she wanted to see Charlie again. He was handsome, super sweet to his niece, and he'd been kind to Jessica as well, despite everything she'd done.

She bundled up and trudged over to Sally's. Ringing the doorbell, she stepped back, waiting for someone to answer.

The door cracked open and Morgan peeked out with a hopeful look on her face—that promptly fell when she saw it was Jessica. "Oh, it's you."

"Can I come in please? I want to talk to your mommy."

Morgan shrugged and let the door swing open. Jessica followed her inside.

"Mommy's sleeping. She worked all night and wants to rest before we go to Grandma's."

"Oh, she must be really tired."

"Yeah, Uncle Charlie is, too, and he promised he'd help me build a snowman. But he fell asleep while he was reading me a story." She crossed her arms and looked down at her feet.

Jessica could see Charlie slumped over the arm of the couch, the book still open on his lap. She was probably asking for trouble, but she knew what she had to do. "I could help you build a snowman."

Morgan's head snapped up. "Really? Right now? You mean it?"

Jessica nodded. "Get your coat and things on, and we'll go outside and make the best snowman ever." She bit her lip. That was probably a bad promise to make, given her track record so far that day.

After getting dressed, Morgan led the way, and they picked a spot out front that wasn't entirely covered in footprints from the night before. Jessica sent up a quick prayer that this was good packing snow and not the fluffy stuff that wouldn't stick together. She scoop up a handful of snow, patted and shaped it between her gloved hands, and smiled. A snowball rested in her palm.

"Okay, Morgan. Now let's roll this little ball in the snow until it's big enough for the snowman base."

Morgan nodded and took the snowball from her, rolling it through the yard. It got bigger and bigger, until Morgan needed help pushing it.

"I think that's good. Now let's make a smaller one for the middle." Jessica handed her another snowball and Morgan made a second ball. A light dusting of snow fell from the sky. The street was perfectly quiet and still. A talented photographer could've turned the scene into a lovely postcard—if they Photoshopped the trampled front yard out of the picture.

"Does this ball look good?" she asked Jessica.

"It looks perfect. Now help me pick it up and put it on top. You grab one side and I'll get the other." Together, they lifted it and set it on top of the bottom. Jessica held out her hand for a high-five. Morgan smiled and slapped her fuzzy wool palm against hers.

"One more for the top," Jessica said.

As Morgan was rolling out the final ball for the head, she turned to look back at Jessica. "There were some cool pages in the coloring book Santa brought. I forgot that coloring can be so much fun."

Jessica felt a huge smile light up her cold cheeks. "I'm glad. I loved coloring when I was little."

Morgan patted the ball she'd made. "I think this is ready. Let me try to put it on top."

"Go for it."

Morgan picked it up and plunked it on the second ball. "We did it!" She ran back to where Jessica was standing and hugged her.

Jessica's throat tightened and she patted Morgan's back.

Morgan looked up at her. "I just wish we had buttons and carrots and stuff to decorate it. Or wouldn't it be cool if we could color it in like it was a coloring book?"

An idea came to Jessica. "Maybe we can. Wait right here." She dashed back to her house and ran into her garage. She scooped up cans of leftover spray paint that she'd been reluctant to throw out. She knew being a packrat would pay off someday. She ran back to Morgan's house and dropped them in the snow. "Let's paint our snowman!"

Morgan's mouth fell open. "Are you serious? We can do that?"

"What, you think someone's going to call the

police?"

Morgan shrugged, like it was a good possibility.

Jessica frowned. "Don't worry. I made a mistake last night." Then, remembering the image of Charlie struggling to get in the window, she fought back a grin. "I heard something that scared me."

Morgan nodded and grabbed a can of red spray paint. "Let's make him look like Santa."

They painted their snowman red and gave him black dots for buttons and eyes. Morgan found a can of green spray paint and spent a long time spelling out "Merry Christmas!" on the front lawn.

"What's all this?" Charlie was standing in the driveway with his hands in his coat pockets.

Jessica was so startled she dropped her can of spray paint. "Hi! I stopped by to talk to Sally, and Morgan was looking for someone to build a snowman with." Jessica looked down at her boots. "You were both sleeping."

"God, I hope I wasn't snoring." He frowned. "Or worse—drooling."

She laughed. "Neither, I promise."

"Uncle Charlie! Look what we did! We made a snowman and we painted it, just like it was a real-life coloring book or something! Come see!" Morgan waved Charlie over for a closer look.

"Nice work. We've got a couple of artists here."

"Do you like the angel I painted?" Morgan pointed to the figure that looked more like a bat than an angel. Then she froze. "Oh. My. Gosh. Uncle Charlie! I think I see hoof prints."

Charlie looked over at Jessica and one side of his mouth curled up. Her heart thumped faster and she wished she could give him a hug. She bit her lip and raised an eyebrow.

He turned back to Morgan. "Really? Show me."

She pointed to one of the few hoof prints left in the snow that hadn't been destroyed by police shoes. She dropped down on her hands and knees for a closer look.

"It is! It really is a hoof print." She stood up and wrapped her hands around Charlie's waist. "You were right. We did see proof he was here."

"Let's go make some hot cocoa for your mommy and then we can show her this beautiful front yard. I've never seen anything like it."

The lump that had been sitting in Jessica's stomach like a hunk of coal since she'd ruined everything the night before was gone. But now she felt out of place. "I've got to get back. My sister's stopping over later."

Charlie walked over and grabbed her hand. "Thanks. You really came through, Jessica," he said softly. He squeezed her fingers and she squeezed back.

She wanted nothing more than to drag him over to her house, mistletoe or not. Instead, she shrugged. "Get her inside so she can enjoy Christmas with her mom." She almost choked on the last word, wondering what it would have been like with her own mother. But the way Charlie stared in her eyes chased that bad feeling away. His look made her feel warm and hopeful. She squeezed his hand again.

Morgan ran to her. "We've got the coolest house on the street now. Thanks, Jessica!"

"It was fun. Maybe we can do it again."

"Can I keep the paint?"

"Sure!" Realizing she was still holding Charlie's hand, she dropped it. "So, Merry Christmas. See you again, sometime." She hoped that didn't come out as awkward as it sounded.

"I sure hope so."

Jessica went home and made herself a mug of hot chocolate, and if she had a candy cane, she would've plunked it in—that's how festive she was finally feeling. She'd made Morgan smile. Maybe the little girl would have a good Christmas after all.

She drew a hot bath, brought in her cocoa and a book, and lit a cinnamon-scented candle. Another holiday touch, how about that? It wasn't what you'd call a typical Christmas, but at least she was feeling better.

Half an hour later, she got out of the tub, applied an expensive, goopy clay-mask to her face that she'd been meaning to use, but never had time for, and popped *It's A Wonderful Life* in the DVD.

The doorbell rang and she wondered why Lindy was so early. She patted the towel wrapped around her head and wiggled her nose as the clay started itching her face. At least Jessica had a good excuse not to join Lindy and Alex.

She opened the door and her stomach tumbled. It wasn't Lindy. She blinked at Charlie and Morgan. "Hello," she said as calmly as she could.

Charlie was doing a bad job stifling a grin. "Hi, I hope we aren't bothering you."

She gripped the door. "No, not at all. I was just catching up on my … my beauty regimen." God, did she really just say that?

"You look funny!" Morgan said.

"Hey, that stuff on her face must help Jessica look as pretty as she does," Charlie told his niece. Then he pushed Morgan in front of him. "We just wanted to bring you these. Even though you can't eat them, we had fun decorating them. Didn't we, Morgan?"

"Yeah, but I really wish we could eat them." Morgan looked at them sadly and offered her the tray.

Cheery snowmen with crooked grins smiled up at her. Ornaments with burnt edges were covered with frosting and mounds of pink sprinkles. Jessica took the tray. "They look great, guys."

Charlie grinned at her. "Just wanted to show you it wasn't a total waste."

"Thanks," she said softly. A tingle zinged from her toes to her nose.

"I hate to run, but we've got to get to my Mom's. Do you want to join us? After you get dressed, of course. There's always tons of food, lots of fun."

"That's really sweet of you. But my sister's coming

over and it's going to take a while for me to get ready."
Her fingers grazed her cheek, now crisp with dried clay.

"I don't think anyone would notice if you came like this."

Morgan laughed.

"Your uncle's a funny guy," Jessica said.

"Well, Merry Christmas. I'll stop by and say hi the next time I'm visiting Sally and Morgan."

"Good. I'd like that. Especially if I don't look like this."

He laughed and waved and as they walked across the street.

She hoped he meant it. She'd love to see Charlie again.

She washed off her mask and dried her hair. Lindy would probably think Jessica was moping around so Jessica got dressed, too—in red, just to show some holiday spirit—when the door bell rang.

She prepared herself for a blast of Christmas cheer. Taking a deep breath, Jessica answered the door.

"Merry Christmas!" Lindy hugged Jessica. "Oh, look at you. I thought you'd be sulking around in your jammies. And not even the cute ones I bought you last year, probably those ratty thermals you like."

Lindy bustled over to the couch with bags of presents. Jessica could see the imaginary glitter swirling in her wake. "Wait till you see what I brought!" In years past, Lindy had brought ridiculously expensive gifts in tiny little boxes from Sublime. This year, she had big bags from Save Land.

Jessica pulled out the beautifully wrapped boxes and was surprised to find outfits from the discount store. Her sister had changed. "These are super cute. Thanks. Your gift card is in my purse. I'll get it in a minute." It probably still had the receipt wrapped around it.

She handed it to Lindy. "I just used up my Starbucks gift card from last Christmas. Perfect timing!"

"Thanks for all this. It's nice, really."

Lindy reached into her purse. "I've got one more thing for you." She pulled out a small rectangular package and handed it to Jessica.

"What's this?"

"Open it."

Once she managed to free the gift from its mounds of curly ribbons, the sprig of mistletoe and the handmade gift tag, she unwrapped a picture frame. She squinted at the picture. A five or six-year-old Lindy sat in front of a tree with a baby in her arms. They were surrounded by presents—and people. Lots and lots of people. She looked up at Lindy. "Was this taken on that Christmas?"

Lindy grinned and nodded. "And all this time I'd been thinking about how the presents made that holiday so special. But when I got the picture out today, I realized that was the only Christmas all our friends and family were with us. And you know Dad grew more distant each year, so the big crowds weren't welcome. But this is really the magic I've been remembering. Being surrounded by so much love." She laughed to herself. "And yeah, for a five-year-old, the presents helped, too. But people are what make it special. And you're never going to feel that if you hole up and hide every holiday, Jessica. So come out with me and Alex tonight."

Jessica sighed. "I get your point. I do. We'll do things differently next year. But I don't want to intrude and ruin the holidays for anyone else this year. I'm just putting this Christmas behind me." She handed the picture to Lindy. "Thanks for coming over. I really appreciate it."

"Keep it. That picture is for you. You had a great Christmas, too, that year. Just look at your big smile! You just don't remember it." She hugged Jessica. "I love you, sis. Don't ever forget that."

Jessica hugged her back, long and hard. "I love you, too, Lindy," she said in a whisper.

Once her sister left, she took the picture into her room and fell asleep with it against her chest.

***

Charlie couldn't stop thinking about Jessica. Uncle Mort was talking to him about the football season, but he was only half paying attention. He wondered if she was home alone. Had she cheered up at all? It didn't seem right for such a beautiful woman—inside and out—to look as sad as she did when he said goodbye to her.

And the story of all those disappointing Christmases just about killed him. He had so many wonderful Christmas memories, but she couldn't remember even one that made her eyes sparkle.

Well, I'm going to change that, he thought, surprising himself. He wanted to make Christmas right. Truthfully, there were dozens of things he wanted to do with her, half of which didn't even involve the bedroom. And it wasn't just that she was beautiful. She was the first woman he'd been attracted to because of her inner qualities.

Uncle Mort snapped his fingers in front of Charlie's face. "What are you daydreaming about? Some girl?"

Charlie grinned. "Yeah, I am. And I have to go see her right now." But first, he needed a little help from Morgan.

***

Jessica woke to the sound of the doorbell. It was dark outside, and she wondered if Lindy and Alex were stopping by. She opened the door and was surprised to see Charlie there. "Hi. What are you doing here?"

"I spotted something strange in your front yard."

She looked at him, concerned.

"Don't worry. Not a robber. Come and look."

She slipped on her coat and boots and followed him down her walkway. He spread his arms wide. "I saw Santa in your front yard. Look!" He pointed to a trail of hoofprints which led to a big wrapped box sat in the middle of the yard. In front of it, someone had painted "Merry Christmas, Jessica!" in the snow.

She couldn't help it. She squealed and twirled

around. Something hard and tight unfurled inside her and she leapt into Charlie's arms without thinking.

He squeezed her back. "Hey, I didn't leave it, Santa did. But I certainly don't mind the hug."

She pressed her cheek against his chest, then looked up at him. "I hate to walk over the hoofprints to get it."

"Go ahead. The reindeer won't mind. Not this time, anyway."

That earned a good-natured whack on the arm. She trudged through the snow and picked up the box wrapped in shiny gold paper. "It's really light," she said, surprised.

"Bring it inside so you can open it."

"Do you want to come in through the door or the window?" she teased.

Now she got a playful shove from him.

She carried the present in front of her, wondering if she'd ever opened such a big gift, imagining all the wonderful things that could be in there. She was excited—seriously excited for the first time in a long time. If it was empty, he'd get a punch in the arm for real. Inside, she kicked off her boots and slid off her coat. Charlie did the same and followed her to the couch.

Her stomach flipped. "Can I open it?"

He paused, like he was thinking. "Maybe you should wait."

"Aww, come on!"

Laughing, he said, "Okay. Go for it."

She ripped off the paper with enough gusto to rival Morgan. Once it was unwrapped, she surprised by what she saw: the box from the Barbie house she'd given Morgan. "You regifted the Barbie house?" Most guys probably didn't know that kind of thing wasn't really allowed.

He crossed his arms, grinning. "Just look inside."

She opened the box flaps. It was empty except for a pile of big, cut-out snowflakes at the bottom. She picked one up and saw that it had writing on it in black marker. "Go to see The Nutcracker," she read aloud. She looked at Charlie, confused.

"Read another one," he said.

She reached in and pulled out another misshaped, handmade snowflake. "Ice skating at downtown rink. What is this?"

He sat on the couch and reached for her hand. "It's my box of Christmas magic for you. These are all the things I want to do with you this winter. Things I hope will be magical and fun for you."

"Really?" That tingle was rushing through her full force now.

He nodded. "And this is on one of the snowflakes, too." He leaned over and brushed his lips against hers. Then he grinned. "It's on quite a few of the snowflakes. Kissing you in front of a fire. Kissing you on New Year's. You're great, Jessica. I've never met anyone like you."

She clutched the snowflake against her heart. "This is the nicest present anyone has ever given me." She could barely get the words out. "And after everything I did."

He wrapped his arms around her. "It's *because* of everything you did. You're wonderful and thoughtful and fun. I never expected someone like you to show up in my life."

"You probably didn't expect the police to show up, either," she said, pouting a bit.

"True enough, but it was a small price to pay to meet you." He took a deep breath. "It's been a rough few years since I split from my ex-girlfriend. And you..." He looked down, then up into her eyes. "I've decided you were my Christmas gift, Jessica."

She didn't think that tingle could grow any stronger, but it did. After another, much longer kiss, he pulled back and stared at her, smiling. "Now that's Christmas magic."

Her smile fell and she leaned against him. "It's

Christmas magic for us, but how's Morgan doing?" She wasn't sure the snowman had been enough to make it up to her.

"She was fine, once she got to my mother's. There were so many people there, she forgot all about the rest of the day's disappointments. She even helped me make these snowflakes, being the little artist and all."

She grinned and reached into the box for another snowflake. "Have a snowball fight?"

"We could go do that right now if you want?"

She shook her head "No, I want to find another one with a kiss on it."

He ran his hand through her hair and brought her head to his. "Whatever you want. It's Christmas, baby."

She let the snowflake fall to the ground. "Not just any Christmas. My best Christmas ever."

"Giving Up Guys"
By Lisa Scott

Lori downed the last of her martini and frowned at the couple next to them at the bar, kissing and cuddling. "People in love shouldn't be allowed to come into nightclubs." She made no attempt to keep her voice down. "Especially hot men with girlfriends." She rolled her eyes as the man twirled a piece of the woman's long blond hair around his finger, totally oblivious to the three women staring them down.

Harper tipped up on her toes for a better look and nodded. "You're right. It should be totally illegal. It's like bringing M&Ms to a chocoholics meeting."

Claire tilted her head, watching them. The couple was now forehead to forehead, nudging their noses. "Oh, my god. They're canoodling."

Harper giggled. "Canoodling. I love that word. What's it mean?"

"It means way too much P.D.A in a bar," Lori said.

"What's P.D.A?" Harper asked.

"That's P.D.A." Claire fluttered her fake eyelashes in amazement as she watched them. "Did he just dump a handful of homemade snowflakes in front of her?"

Lori nodded. "He just picked up one that said, *Kiss you on New Year's Eve* in magic marker. And he kissed her." She pretended to stick her finger down her throat.

Claire waved the bartender over. "We need a round of lonely-tinis."

A tall, dark-haired guy walked over and started clearing away their empties. "Sorry, not familiar with that one."

"Of course not. I just made it up. Give us a shot of vodka, Champagne and sad, sad, Blue Curacao and then a dash of our miserable, single girl tears to top it off."

Claire swiped her hand along her forehead for affect.

The bartender fought back a grin. "We don't usually do made up drinks, but I'll make an exception since you lovely ladies are celebrating the new year."

"It's more like man-bashing than celebrating, but thanks." She winked and turned back to her friends, still bemoaning men.

"I'm so sick of wanting that," Lori said, jerking her thumb over her shoulder at the couple, "and instead, getting, 'Hey baby, just cleaned the back seat of my truck. Wanna check it out?'"

"Or, 'Hey, I'm looking for a bed-buddy, you in?'" Claire said. "And let me tell you, girls, I'm cleaning up the language on that one."

Lori nodded in sympathy. "We spend way too much time worrying about guys, and if they're going to call, and why we haven't met any good ones. I wasted three perfectly good months with Ted. Talk-with-his-mouth-full Ted. I could've learned knitting in that time. Or taken CPR classes. Or had a really clean apartment. And Harper, you could've gotten another degree in the year you spent with Liam."

Harper fluffed her long hair, currently dyed a pinkish-red. "You're right. I've been thinking about something in the engineering field. Just for fun. I wouldn't have to shave my legs for *that.*"

Claire smacked the top of the bar. "I spent all that money on fancy lingerie for Spencer—and I can't stand the stuff. You'd think he would've been happy that I sleep naked. He thought it wasn't hygienic."

The bartender looked up from the drink he was pouring. The vodka missed the glass.

"I'm so glad your bustiers aren't hanging out to dry in our shower anymore," Harper said. "It was not fun being your roommate while Spencer was around. I actually caught him cleaning the bathroom once. He used all our bleach wipes."

"At least he didn't haul her off across the country.

Look what Ryan did to Ginny," Lori said. "Dragged her down to Florida. We should be the four musketeers out here tonight." She sighed and adjusted the strap on her sparkly purple dress.

"I miss Ginny. But at least they're engaged. I think she's really happy down there now." Claire tucked a stray piece of blond hair back in her updo.

"Well, she found one of the mythical, good ones—as rare as a five-digit prime number. That's one out of four in our group. What are the chances the rest of us will find a great guy? I've haven't seen the studies, but I'm sure the numbers aren't good," Harper said, wagging her finger at them.

Lori nodded. "You're right. Most guys are irresponsible and disappointing."

"And they're also…" Harper flapped her hands as she searched for just the right word. "Jerks! Things haven't changed since I was five. Boys are dumb." She crossed her arms with a satisfied nod.

"And you're a PhD, so you'd know," Lori said.

The bartender dropped off their drinks and Claire passed them out to the girls. She raised hers to the ceiling. "That's it, ladies. We're giving up guys. That's our New Year's resolution."

Harper froze, wide-eyed. "Giving them up?" She gulped. "Like, cold turkey?"

"Not even a quick hookup?" Claire looked like someone was taking away her coffee for a year. "What if Johnny Depp shows up in town?"

Lori sighed. "Not forever, but for a while. We're better off without them."

Claire set her drink down. "Wait. Last year you resolved to gain weight so that you'd actually lose it—"

"Since resolutions never work," Harper finished. "Hey, didn't you end up losing six pounds? So you were right…" She twisted her lips and narrowed one eye. "Does this mean we're giving up guys so that we'll actually meet them?" She tilted her head as if the weight

131

of it was too much. If it wasn't a math problem, Harper sometimes had a hard time figuring it out.

Lori waved away the idea. "No, we're taking a break from men. If you had a sprained ankle, you wouldn't go running on it. Well, we've got sprained hearts. So we're going to focus on other things we should be doing instead of worrying about men."

"Like cleaning your apartment?" Harper asked.

"No, fun stuff. Stuff we've always wanted to do, but haven't had time to do because of boyfriends and dating," Claire said.

"Like thinning out my closet," Harper said, pouting. "I have way too many camisoles."

Lori sighed. "No, like classes or hobbies."

"What are you going to do?" Claire asked.

Lori looked up at the ceiling, thinking. She snapped her fingers. "I'm going to take an upholstery class."

Claire laughed. "Oooh, you wild thing," she shrieked over the music.

"Hey, it's something I've always wanted to do. I've got several old pieces of gorgeous furniture from my grandma, and I'm sure there will be no hot men in class to distract me. And what about you, Claire?"

"Tough to beat furniture stripping. Maybe I'll take a stripping class, too—the-take-off-your-clothes kind, not just old velvet from some chair."

Harper whacked Claire. "You'll be meeting men for sure if you do that."

Claire fixed her gaze on Harper. "Well, what about you?"

Harper tipped up her chin. "I'll take a class, too."

Lori laughed. "You take classes all the time. Ever since you were in Montessori at age three. Try something new."

"I'm going to take a belly dancing class. Men don't belly dance, so I'll be perfectly safe. And it'll be a blast." She shimmied her hips and waved her hands over her head for an impromptu preview.

Claire gave her an amused look. "You look like a dying snake. You could use the help."

Harper pouted and flopped back on her stool. "What about you? How about pole vaulting instead of pole dancing?"

Claire made a face.

"What have you always wanted to do?" Lori asked.

Claire crossed her arms and sighed. "Scuba diving?"

"That would be fun," Lori said.

"The community college offers scuba diving lessons all the time." Harper clapped and Claire shrugged in agreement.

"Looks like we have a plan, ladies." Lori raised her glass in the air again. "To giving up guys!"

"Hear, hear!" said Harper and Claire.

They downed their drinks and Lori flagged down the bartender again.

"Another round of lonely-tinis?" he asked.

She looked at him like he was crazy. "No. We need Champagne now, to celebrate being single," Lori said.

"We're giving up guys!" Claire informed him.

"Champagne with a cherry, since we won't be popping ours anytime soon!" Harper said.

Claire dropped her head in her hands. "You did that a long time ago, honey."

Harper shrugged, confused. "But we're giving up guys!"

Lori patted her on the back. "That's right, honey, we are."

"But weren't the lonely-tinis because you're sad to be single?" the bartender asked.

"Blame it on a mood swing, but we're happy to be single, now, so bring out the bubbly!" Claire demanded.

The bartender sighed and shrugged, and walked over to grab a bottle of champagne. "Not a bad idea. I think I'll give up women for a while," he mumbled to himself.

After he dropped off their drinks, the ladies raised another toast, but they were distracted by the couple next to them—now making out.

"Get a room!" Lori called.

The couple looked their way, giggled, and hurried toward the exit.

"Yay! No guys. I can't wait!" Harper said.

Claire cleared her throat. "How long are we doing this for?"

"At least a month. You know, really get guys out of our systems. How about we resolve to stay single until Valentine's Day? We'll meet out on February 14th and talk about how much fun we've been having. Deal?"

"Deal," Harper and Claire said together, clinking their glasses with Lori.

***

When Lori woke up after lunch the next day, she winced, vowing never to drink lonely-tinis again. She hopped on the internet and found a few upholstery classes starting in January. There were several, and she chose the one closest to her at the local high school. She printed out the supply list, excited for the new adventure that started later that week. "Six weeks with out guys," she said to her dog, Buster. "Except for you, of course." She rubbed his head and he rolled over onto his belly. "If all guys were this loveable, I wouldn't be doing this."

That Thursday night, she changed into old sweatpants and a flannel shirt, and loaded Grandma Miller's claw-foot chair into her backseat. She brought along the fabric she'd selected and her tools and supplies. It was turning into an expensive little venture, but she was excited for the challenge; something just for her that had nothing to do with men. The class was being held in the cafeteria, so she made two trips carrying in her things, pleased to see mostly women assembled in the room, along with two older men.

However, the women were wearing front-of-the-closet-stuff. She frowned at her bottom-of-the-dresser-drawer wardrobe. Then she shrugged it off. What did it matter what she looked like? This was the kind of thinking she was trying to change.

She was laying out her tools when the chatter stopped, and the women focused their attention to the front of the room, where a man was setting down his things at the first table. Giddy whispers passed between the women, and Lori took a second look at the him. *Robert Redford meets Kevin Costner,* she thought to herself. She'd assumed the guy teaching the class would be older and unattractive, not a movie star stunt double.

That explained why the women looked like they were off to happy hour instead of an adult education class. For a moment, her imagination went wild, picturing a lewd moment with the man on an unfinished couch. She closed her eyes and shook it off. *I'm here for the furniture, not teacher-eye-candy.*

The instructor introduced himself. "I'm Tom Murphy from the Take Cover upholstery shop in town. And tonight we're going to strip."

That got some laughter and hoots. "I recognize some familiar faces. I'm glad to see so many of you taking the class again. Let's review the steps for re-upholstering a piece of furniture, then you can get to work removing the old fabric, and I'll come around and take a look at what you're all working on." His grin was mesmerizing, even when she was sitting at the back of the room. Well, she was not going to be taken in by him. She had to build up her immunity to uber-hotties. She focused on her chair and removing the old brocade fabric.

Nervous giggles and chatter followed Tom as he made the rounds. Lori rolled her eyes at the ridiculousness, as she struggled to remove the faded material. She was swearing to herself when Tom approached her table. She didn't stop working.

"Nice piece," he said.

She looked up and got lost for a moment in his amber eyes. Apparently, giving up guys would be a baby-step process. She blew out a deep breath and looked back at her chair. "Thanks. Family heirloom. No pressure, right?"

He laughed and smoothed his hands along the legs—the chair's, not hers. But she wouldn't have minded. He was nearing forty, with sandy blond hair dashed with a bit of gray; one of those guys who gets cuter with time, and older than anyone she'd ever dated. Didn't matter though. She wouldn't be dating him.

"These legs should be refinished before you start." Somehow, his voice made him even more handsome.

Lori groaned. "I don't know how to do that. Is it hard?"

He handed her a card. "Stop by my workshop with the chair before next week's class and I'll show you."

She grinned. "Thanks." And that was not a date; it was a business appointment. *Look at me—totally following my resolution.*

***

Harper tried once more to move her hips to the left, and then reverse them to the right, but she kept stumbling, while the dozen or so women around her were getting the hang of it immediately, moving like Egyptian goddesses.

Vivienne, the tiny sixty-something instructor, smiled kindly at her, coming over and setting her hands on Harper's hips, gently guiding her movements. "Relax, let it come to you. You'll get the hang of it." She patted Harper's hip.

"Thanks." Harper tried to let her body move with the mesmerizing music, but it wasn't cooperating. It was ridiculous. She should be able to move in time with the music, and follow the beat. *There's math involved, just count out the beats! It's like a moving math problem.* She wondered if it too late to join Claire for scuba lessons. Jutting her hip to the left and stumbling a bit, she realized everyone else had stopped dancing. *Am I that bad?*

But everyone in the room was staring towards the

door. A tall, dark-haired guy stood there, rubbing the back of his head while he studied his feet.

Vivienne smiled at him. "Are you Patrick?"

He looked up at her and forced a smile. "Yes, I am."

"Excellent. You're my first male student. I thought maybe your registration was a joke."

He laughed. "More like a lost bet."

"Well, we're happy to have you here. Join us and come back here. I'll show you what you've missed."

Patrick walked to the back of the room and took the spot next to Harper. He smiled at her, and she gave him a quick grin, before looking down. She was certain she was blushing like an eleven-year-old caught gawking at her lab partner.

"Alright, let's begin again. Roll your hips like a figure eight. Patrick, follow my moves." Vivienne stood in front of him and rolled her hips.

Patrick took a deep breath, set his hands on his hips and jerked through the movements. Harper fought back a grin. It was nice no longer being the worst student in class. Patrick grimaced and looked over at her. He laughed and shook his head.

Vivienne walked behind him and guided his hips just like she had with Harper. Unlike Harper, though, he was actually getting the hang of it once Vivienne showed him the way. Harper stopped dancing and crossed her arms, watching him.

He looked over and shrugged. "Lord of the Dance. Who knew?"

Vivienne went back to the front of the room and told the group to stop for a water break. "Thank god," Harper whispered.

"What, did you lose a bet, too?" Patrick asked her.

She laughed. "No, this was all my idea. My girlfriend's and I decided to…" Nibbling her lip, she was reluctant to admit she'd had such bad luck with men that she was giving them up for a while. She felt like a tipsy college student taking a break from all-night keggers. "We all decided to try something new for our New Year's resolution. And I picked belly dancing lessons." She sighed. "Let's just say I'm not a natural."

"Wow, so you did this on purpose." He shook his head. "I lost a bet on New Year's, and here I am. Apparently, I can't drink like I could back in my college days." He held out his hand. "Patrick Dunn."

"Harper Reese." Her fingertips tingled as she shook his hand. "So, are you taking all six weeks of classes?"

He shrugged, looking her up and down. "It's not as bad as I thought. I'll be back next week. I'm pretty sure the guys at the office have a bet on how long I'll last. What about you?"

She twisted her fingers behind her back. "I figure my friends will be expecting a belly dancing recital or something. I've got to come back."

He grinned. "Glad to hear it."

Feeling a flush creep up her neck, Harper snapped her head away and Vivienne called the class back to order. When the music started again, she peeked at Patrick; then stumbled to the side, right into him.

He steadied her with big hands wrapped around her waist. If this were *Dirty Dancing*, he'd pick her up and spin her around over his head. She stepped back from him at that thought; it certainly wouldn't end well. She was a feet-on-the-floor kind of girl. But still, being in his arms was nice. She sucked in a breath and resumed her pathetic flailing about.

It seemed that belly dancing class had just gotten ten times harder with Patrick around.

And just as exciting.

***

Claire admired her new one-piece bathing suit in the locker room mirror before she headed out to the pool area. Jumping into the pool with a bikini could lead to a wardrobe malfunction, and you never knew who was lurking around with a cell phone camera, looking to upload the next viral YouTube video.

She hadn't worn a one-piece since she spent her childhood summers in her friend Ginny's backyard pool playing Marco Polo. Then she tried to remember the last time she'd actually gone swimming at the beach, and her memories were reaching back to the pre-teen years. No matter. She could totally do this.

Walking out into the pool area, she was pleased to see no hot men had registered for the course. There was a husband and wife, preparing for a Caribbean vacation, two women in their fifties, and a couple of geeky college guys eyeing her up. Another good reason to have opted for the one-piece.

The course was highly rated online, and she was eager to meet their instructor, a retired Navy SEAL in his sixties; no threat to the resolution, there. Stan Worthington introduced himself to the group, showed them the equipment they'd be using and would have to buy or rent before the third lesson, and then lined them up for the required swimming skills test.

"I need to see that you can tread water for ten minutes, swim two-hundred yards—your choice of stroke—and swim the length of the pool underwater without coming up for air.

Claire's hand shot in the air and wiggled her fingers. "Excuse me?"

"Yes?" Stan didn't sound pleased to have been interrupted.

"I didn't see that mentioned in the course description. Are you sure that's a requirement? Underwater all the way?"

"It's a requirement in my class. If you can't swim underwater the length of the pool, you have no business being scuba diving in the ocean."

Claire gulped and nodded. When she and Ginny had hold-your-breath-underwater contests, Ginny had always won. And Ginny was two years younger!

Suddenly, she realized a wardrobe malfunction was the least of her worries.

Claire stood at the end of the line, watching each student dive in and swim to the other length of the pool, no sweat. Her heart sped up as her turn approached. She took swimming lessons a few times at the rec. center one summer. *You can do this, you can do this.*

Finally, it was her turn. Standing in front of the pool with her toes curling over the edge, she took a deep breath and dove in, although it felt more like a belly flop. Her chest was tight as she pulled herself through the water with some sort of under-water breast-stroke. She didn't know how far she'd gotten before her lungs felt like they would burst, but she knew she wasn't at the end. Her head popped up out of the water and she heard a whistle blow as she gasped for air.

"You're going to have to try that again next week," the teacher shouted.

She was distracted for the rest of the class, not paying close attention to the safety protocols he was reviewing. As the students filed toward the locker room, the teacher stopped her. "Listen, if you can't pass that swim test, I can't certify you. And there will be a quiz on the safety steps I went through today. I can see you've got yourself a pretty new bathing suit, but this isn't a pool party. You need to pay attention."

Claire felt her cheeks redden. "Okay, sir. Yes, sir." Feeling like a delinquent high-school teen, she scuttled off to the locker room. She changed, blow dried her hair until it was just damp, and decided she needed a drink.

She stopped off at the club where they'd spent New Year's Eve. The same bartender was there, and she hoped he didn't remember her; they'd been a tad obnoxious that night, as far as she could recall.

She sat down at the bar and he slid a cocktail napkin in front of her. "Are you up for another lonely-tini?"

She wrinkled her nose. "So you remember that. No, I need more of a drown-my-sorrows-tini." Although drown probably wasn't the best word after her performance in the pool. "Something to wash down embarrassment and regret." Because even after one lesson, she was regretting the deal she'd made with the girls. She remembered quite vividly now she did not like to swim and that she did like men—a lot. Especially men with pale blue eyes and dark hair, like the bartender smiling at her.

He rubbed his chin. "Embarrassment and regret. I've got just the thing for you—only if you tell me what's got you embarrassed and full of regret."

She rested her chin in her hand. "I signed up for scuba diving lessons, and I hate it. I can't swim very well, and my instructor is this mean Navy SEAL dude."

"So quit."

She put her hands on her hips, imitating her mother's voice as well as she could. "The Penningtons aren't quitters. Try and try again, that's our motto." She rolled her eyes. "Plus my friends and I all made this New Year's resolution to try new things instead of..." She shrugged and let her sentence trail off, embarrassed to admit what they'd agreed to.

But he finished the sentence for her. "Give up guys, right?"

Her eyes widened. "How did you know?"

He laughed. "You toasted to it, like, five times." He shrugged and wiped down the bar. "Plus, you inspired me to give up women for a while."

She raised an eyebrow. "Really? Sounds like there's a good story there."

He shrugged. "No different than yours, I'm sure. I'm just sick of the scene, being disappointed when relationships go nowhere. It's a big relief, actually."

"You think so? I'm counting down the days until it's over, believe me."

He leaned against the bar. "You think you can

last?"

"If I don't drown in scuba class, first."

He smiled and her knees felt weak even though she wasn't standing. Sitting across from a hot guy at a bar was a bad place to be for a gal giving up guys.

He held out his hand. "Nate Johnson, and I'm here every Thursday if you'd rather jump into a martini than the pool."

She raised an eyebrow and shook his hand. "Claire Pennington, and that's good to know. I have a feeling I'm going to get to know you well."

***

Lori wandered into Tom's re-upholstering workshop two days before her next class. It was located right next to her favorite flower shop in town, Your Heart's Desire. She wondered how often Your Heart's Desire had to make deliveries to their handsome neighbor next door. He was chatting with a customer, and his smile blew her away from across the room. If she hadn't given up guys, she would totally be preparing a flirty line or two.

Instead, she blew out her breath, shook off the lusty feelings and carried her chair over to him. She looked around at furniture in all different states of completion. It looked like business was booming for him, and she'd bet a bundle most of his customers were women.

"So, I have no idea how to strip," she said, turning red as she realized how that sounded. "The wood, I mean. Strip the wood." She coughed. "The wood." Man, now she was turning redder.

He was gracious enough not to laugh. "It's not too hard." Now his cheeks were turning pink. He shook it off. "Let me show you, so you can do it yourself next time. You can use a chemical remover, but I like to use a disc sander. You've got to be careful, though, not to damage the wood."

He turned on a small sander and buzzed it quickly over the legs, removing most of the stain. "Now we're going to go over this with fine sandpaper. Let me show you the proper technique."

"Okay. I'm all about technique." The words came out in a sexy tone. She gritted her teeth. Was she programmed to automatically flirt with a handsome man? Was she helpless to stop?

He looked at her. "Glad to hear it. Technique's important for a lot of things." He gave her a piece of sandpaper, and set his hand over hers, guiding it along, moving with the grain of the wood. She hated how nice his hand felt on top of hers. His hand was big and strong, and the tips of his fingers felt rough. That would be an interesting sensation along her stomach, or her inner thigh.

She closed her eyes and tried to fight the feeling.

He let her finish the final leg, and she took a step back, admiring her work. "Beautiful, " he said, but he wasn't looking at the chair; he was staring at her. Then he checked his watch. "It's just about closing time. Let's get the stain on this, and then would you like to join me for dinner? I can tell you all about webbing stretchers."

That would be important to know, she told herself. Sort of like extra credit and not at all like a date. A field trip. Yes, that's what it was. "Sure. I need to know all I can about webbing stretchers."

***

They lingered over burgers and shakes at the diner down the street, laughing and talking until the waitress practically shooed them out into the snowy night.

She discovered that they both loved horror films, golden retrievers, and stout beer—and they did actually talk about webbing stretchers. For two minutes. When he walked her to her car, she realized there was definitely a spark between them. But she took a step back. "Thanks, Tom. That was fun."

He shoved his hands in his pockets. "I can give

you a personal lesson on channel tins this Saturday if you're interested." It was probably a reupholstering term, but the way he said it made her shiver.

Man, no wonder all his students returned for a second session. She frowned. "I'm sorry, I can't." She wasn't about to explain why she couldn't, and she wasn't about to break the girls' resolution. It had been her idea, for crying out loud.

He looked surprised, then resigned. "Okay. I'll bring your chair to class. See you in a few days, Lori."

***

Vivienne handed out flashy gold-coin belts to the belly dancing class. "Now you can hear your hips shaking. A little inspiration to get your groove on."

That just didn't sound right coming from sweet little Vivienne. Harper tied hers on and swished her hips. Patrick waltzed past her with an exaggerated sexy sway, his gold coins clinking against each other.

"Show off," Harper teased. "Are your friends shocked you came back for another lesson?"

"I think they were considering joining when I told them about all the hot women in class."

"I don't think you could handle Vivienne," she teased.

"Redheads are more my speed," he said, staring at her hair.

She hoped her face wasn't turning a similar color. Luckily, the music started and she turned away from him.

At the end of the class, she tried to hurry to her car and avoid any more flirty talk with him. She would not break this resolution. But Patrick caught up to her. "Hey, wanna grab a drink?"

Harper shivered, even though she'd buttoned up her winter coat. "I can't." She stomped her boots in the snow.

"Oh, sorry. Do you have a boyfriend?"

She shoved her hands in her pockets. "No, it's just not a good time."

He took a step back. "Okay. Be sure to let me know when it is."

Her breath came out a steamy puff in the air. "Oh."

***

The scuba instructor pulled Claire aside after class. "This is the second week you've failed the swim test. Are you going to try again next week, or do you want your money back?"

What else would she do with this stupid one-piece bathing suit? But then she thought about getting her two-hundred-dollar class fee back, and all the money she'd save not renting scuba gear. She'd be happy just snorkeling on her next Caribbean vacation—whenever that was going to be. She held out her hand. "Let's not waste anyone else's time. I want out."

He patted her on the back. "I think that's the best decision for all of us."

She didn't want to go home and face Harper, who was bound to have eighty questions about her class, so she found herself back at the bar. Nate smiled when he saw her. "Ah, its my favorite fish swimming by for a visit."

Claire pouted. "Give me a quit-tini. The instructor strongly suggested I leave the class and get my money back."

"Ouch. Sorry to hear it. But I am glad you're drowning your sorrows here." He started mixing a drink for her while she pouted; it certainly wasn't her best look, but it didn't matter, did it? She wasn't looking to hook up with a guy, not even a hot, friendly, funny guy.

"I feel terrible. I'm totally letting the girls down. We were supposed to learn something fun and new. The only thing I learned is that I'm a terrible swimmer and probably too old for something fun and new." She stirred her rum and Coke with the red swizzle stick. "Plus, if I don't go to class my roommate will know I dropped out. I'll never hear the end of it."

"Come here instead. How will they ever know you dropped out? It's not like there's a scuba graduation, right? How would you ever keep the cap on in the pool?" He slid a new drink in front of her.

"True. You willing to put up with me every Thursday for a while?"

"It'll be the highlight of my week."

Mine too.

When Claire got home, Harper was waiting for her. She closed the giant book she was reading. "How was class?"

"Great. Super fun. Wish I'd done it years earlier." She gave Harper a great big smile. That was probably a dead giveaway that she was lying.

Harper cocked her head. "Why isn't your hair wet?"

"Oh, they have hair dryers there."

Harper nodded, tapping her fingers on the book cover. "How are you doing with no man action?"

Claire went into the kitchen and grabbed a soda from the fridge. "Fine. I'm fine. It's not a problem at all." She pressed the can against the back of her neck.

"I know. It's a huge relief, really. I'm so glad we did this."

The two of them stared at each other, smiling.

"Can't wait to hear how Lori's doing," Claire said.

"Maybe we'll decide on Valentine's to keep this up," Harper suggested.

Claire felt her smile waver. "Who knows?"

***

At the end of the third class, Tom asked Lori to wait. The few women still left—taking their time packing up, probably hoping for a minute alone with their teacher—quickly gathered their things and trudged out into the night.

Lori's heart kicked up a notch as she walked up to him. "What's up?"

He piled up some papers and looked up at her.

"There's a new movie opening this weekend. *Saw 15*, I think. Want to go see it?"

"Yes," she said before realizing she was agreeing to a date.

His grin was huge. "Great."

Well, she couldn't back out of it now, could she?

"Let's go grab a drink. Want to meet over at Vibe?"

The original site of her resolution to ditch men for a while? Major guilt trip, but she could handle it. Guys like Tom were as rare as a mint-condition Chippendale camelback sofa. Plus, she was learning so much from him about antiques and refinishing furniture. She'd be signing up for a second class for sure. "Sounds good."

The phone rang as Lori followed Tom to the bar. She grabbed it without looking. "Hello?"

"Lori, it's Harper. Want to meet me and Claire out for a drink? Your class is over, right? We're going to Vibe."

She almost drove off the road. "Right now?"

"Yeah, we're heading there right now."

"I can't. I..." She sucked in a deep breath, searching for an adequate lie. "I totally screwed up the tufting on the back of my chair, and the teacher is nice enough to help me redo it."

"That's the old guy you told us about?"

"Yeah, he's old." She had twisted the truth just a bit when they'd asked about class. "Really old and cranky."

"Bummer. We wanted to catch up. We're still on for Valentine's right?"

"Of course. Just the girls." Lori hung up and followed Tom into the parking lot. How was she going to get out of this?

He got out and opened her door for her. She stood up, just inches away from him. She shivered as a freezing gust blew past. Oh, how nice it would be cuddled up in his arms. "Listen, I'm not really in the mood for a noisy bar tonight."

He raised an eyebrow. "We could have a drink at my place. I don't live far away. And I could show you the Chippendale set I refinished."

Well, this was in the name of re-upholstering education, wasn't it? "Perfect. I'll follow you there." She wasn't sure, but she swore she saw Harper's car pulling into the lot as she was pulling out. She scrunched down in her seat.

Patrick's place was a beautiful old colonial with stained glass windows, crown molding, and gorgeous furniture. He came out of the kitchen with two glasses of wine as she wandered around his living room.

She took the drink from him and swallowed a healthy gulp. Her hand shook a bit holding the glass. "It's such a fantastic place and so many beautiful pieces of furniture."

"Thanks. My ex hated antiques." He laughed. "Not sure how we ended up together. Have you ever been married?"

She took another long drink. "No. Not even close."

"I find that hard to believe."

"It's true what they say: good men are hard to find."

He took a step closer. "So are mint Art Deco chairs, but they're out there." The way he smiled at her made her stomach flip.

She sat down on the couch and he sat next to her. This was too much to ask, resisting this handsome, interesting man.

He set down his wine and it was like their lips were drawn to each other. He snaked his hand through her hair and kissed her. It was a soft, warm, passionate kiss, but she pulled back, catching her breath. "Maybe I shouldn't kiss my teacher. I wouldn't want it to affect my grade."

He laughed. "There are no grades in my class." He pulled her to him and kissed her again. This time, she didn't hesitate in kissing him back. She pushed her friends' disappointed reactions out of her mind. How was she going to face them now?

***

By the fourth week, it was clear that Patrick was actually a very good belly dancer. Since you danced with your knees bent, like you were trying to sit on a chair, the best dancers had strong legs. And Patrick appeared to have very strong legs. He was totally the best shimmier in class and he wasn't afraid to flaunt it.

He caught her checking him out several times during the class, and she snapped her gaze away, certain she could hear him chuckling.

"I'm just trying to follow your moves," she whispered to him one of the times he caught her eye.

He danced closer to her. "I can give you private lessons if you think it'd help."

That sent her heart rate up higher than the dancing.

When the class finally ended, Patrick lingered, taking his time gathering his things. She did the same, until it was just them and the teacher.

Vivienne struggled to hold back a sly grin. "You two can stay and practice if you'd like."

"Excellent idea. I think we will," Patrick said.

Vivienne slipped out of the room and Harper sucked in a deep breath. "You really don't have to."

He crossed his arms, and his muscles bulged. "You're right. But I want to." He took a step closer. "Then I can demand a private recital when the class is over. Or at least invitation to the one you're giving your friends."

She gulped and nodded. "I'm not sure you can help me. If you haven't noticed I'm pretty pathetic. When I'm doing my ribcage circles, I look like I'm convulsing. I'm surprised no one has called 911."

He laughed. "But your arm waves aren't bad."

"You're just being nice. Plus, Vivienne took the music with her. This probably won't work."

"Not a problem. Maybe the music's distracting you."

That's not what's distracting me. Truth was though, she'd been horrible even before he'd shown up in class.

He came up behind her, and his fingers hovered over her hips. "May I?"

She nodded, and he placed his hands on her hips. She stiffened. "Don't worry," he whispered.

Letting out a breath, she tried to be not so rigid. "Okay. Now what?"

"Close your eyes."

That only made her widen her eyes. "Why?"

"Just do it."

She closed her eyes, and Patrick slowly moved her hips in a figure eight. His chest grazed her back, and that set her heart pounding. She was stiff and resistant at first. This wasn't breaking the resolution, was it? It was tutoring.

Then she felt his lips brush her ear. "Relax. I have a feeling you haven't done that in a while."

She blew out a long breath. "You're right." She felt her shoulders ease, and let herself be moved by Patrick's hands. Slowly, he took his hands away. "Keep going," he told her.

Her hips kept moving in the same rhythm. Her eyes flew open. "I'm doing it!" Feeling brave, she added an arm wave, and started moving across the room.

"You look great!" He waited until she got closer, grabbed one of her hands, and pulled her to him.

She didn't resist. He twirled her in an impromptu dance and then dipped her. When he pulled her back up, she was face to face with him. He swiped his lips across hers. "Please tell me now is a good time."

She exhaled, then frowned.

So did he, dropping her hand. "If it's not a

boyfriend, then what is it?"

"Remember how I told you for New Year's my friends and I resolved to try new things?"

"Yeah."

"Well, we also resolved to give up guys. Until Valentine's Day."

"Seriously?"

She nodded.

"That's only a few weeks away. Does that mean you'll go out with me on Valentine's?"

She could meet the girls afterward for a drink after their date and fess up. After all, they did say until Valentine's Day. "Absolutely."

"Great. My sister owns this flower shop and they're having this make your own arrangement and dinner event. She wanted me to go, but I told her I didn't have a date. But now I do. She'll be thrilled."

Harper's eyes widened. "I don't think my flower arranging is going to be any better than my dancing. I'm a mathematician. Numbers and facts? Sure. The creative stuff? Not so much."

"A mathematician. What do you do?"

"I work for the government. I'd have to kill you if I told you exactly what I do. Well, it probably wouldn't be me killing you; but I think they have people for that." She twisted her lips. "Unless my boss was kidding. He does like to play jokes on me"

He laughed. "I'll take my chances. You can be in charge of counting the flowers." He kissed her again. "Want to grab something to eat?"

Backing away, she shook her head. "We have to wait."

He held up his arms in surrender and laughed. "Okay. Then let's keep practicing." He wrapped his arms around her this time, and they moved together in a slow figure eight hip roll that was the sexiest damn thing she'd done in a long time.

***

With two weeks left in the scuba class she was no longer taking, Claire was actually looking forward to her visits with Nate. This was the longest time she'd ever spent talking to a guy and getting to know him without kissing him. Or more. Usually more.

Inspired by their lonely-tini, he'd been trying new drinks on her to use as new specials. "Today we've got the lust-tini."

She caught his eye and smiled. The week before it had been the smitten-tini. "I can't wait to see what you come up with next week."

"They're selling well, I can tell you that. Probably because they're inspired."

"I'd say the flirt-tini should be next, if you're going for inspired drinks."

"But they're all inspired by you. Just you."

She took this week's drink from him and sipped it, closing her eyes. "Nice. The taste really lingers." She set the drink down. "Just how long are you intending to give up women? We're only doing this until Valentine's Day. That's when I'm back on the market." She blinked at him. "If you know what I mean." She rubbed the condensation on her glass. "Or, maybe I could end a little early. The girls wouldn't have to know."

"But I'd know. No, we'll wait until Valentine's Day."

Claire took another drink. "So, you want to do something on Valentine's?"

"I've got to work, of course. But we could go out late."

Truth was, she didn't really want to go anywhere but his place. She didn't need a long, romantic dinner to get to know him better, to decide if he was kissing material—or more. She already knew that. In the four weeks they'd been visiting for a few hours on Thursdays, she'd learned that he thought he could be a vegetarian if he didn't like meat so much. He totally understood her guilt over enjoying steak. He hated camping, which was great news, because she wouldn't be sleeping in the woods for anyone, killer blue eyes or not. And when he told her he loved cats—Siamese cats in particular, and her favorite—she knew this guy was more than fling material.

She sighed. "Okay, so it's agreed. Nothing more than talking until Valentine's Day."

He looked at her and raised an eyebrow. "You won't regret it."

"We're actually meeting here that night, since that's where we planned this whole damn thing, so pretend we haven't been mentally undressing each other the past few weeks."

"I hate to tell you this, but I've mentally been doing more than that."

She reached over to whack him but missed. "Alright, since you're keeping our relationship in your head until then, give me an agony-tini."

He laughed. "How about a worth-the-wait-tini."

"Just give me a drink—since you won't give me anything else."

***

Lori couldn't help it. She'd been seeing Tom before class, after class, and several days in between classes. How was she going to admit this to the girls after telling them her teacher was an old cranky guy?

They sat in front of his fireplace, leafing through a photo album of furniture he'd refinished. "Do you want to go to some estate sales with me when the class is over? We could look for your next piece to refinish."

She leaned against him. "That would be great." Would she have to admit to him some day that she'd broken her own resolution? She wasn't sure what he'd think. She felt guilty, but her feelings for him certainly overshadowed that.

"What are we going to do for Valentine's Day?"

She smiled at his question. There didn't seem to be any doubt in his mind that they were a couple. But how was she going to explain that she had plans with her friends that night? She couldn't exactly call them and say, 'Sorry, I'm going out with my secret boyfriend.'

He set down his wine. "Do you not want to go out on Valentine's Day?"

"I do. But I had promised my girlfriends we'd go out. They don't have boyfriends."

"That's okay. I understand. But could you stop my shop before you meet them out? I've got a present there for you for Valentine's Day."

"A present for me? I think I can squeeze you in. I'm just not sure what to get you."

He kissed her. "Nothing. You're present enough."

Oh, she was so glad she broke her resolution.

**

Harper tried not to check the clock too often. She was meeting the girl's at nine, and their flowers-and-dinner affair at Your Heart's Desire had started at six-thirty. Patrick's sister, Lynn, was thrilled he'd brought a date, especially since it was the first time they'd tried something like this. Lynn's new worker, Marnie, had come up with the plan, and she and her boyfriend were dressed up as cupids as they wandered around serving drinks and hors d' oeuvres. The whole thing was quite fun.

She'd been right that flower arranging wasn't her thing, but Patrick had amused her by chomping on a rose and waltzing her around the room. She tried to keep up and ended up laughing and collapsing in her seat.

"At least I didn't make you belly dance." He looked at her and winked. "Later."

Their dinner of surf and turf was lovely, and he'd fed her the lobster tail he didn't want. They were quickly lapsing into a sickening sweet couple and it was all because they were so desperate to kiss. She was impressed by her will power.

When dinner finally ended, Harper hugged Lynn and thanked her for a fabulous time. She heard Lynn whisper to Patrick, "She's a keeper."

They held hands and handed for the door. "This is the part where I turn into a pumpkin. It's time to meet my friends out."

"And then after that, you're all mine," Patrick said, moving in for a kiss.

Harper dodged out of the way. "Not yet!"

***

Lori had brought a big box of Truffles and a bottle of Tom's favorite wine to his shop. The wine was finished, and they'd put a good dent in the chocolate. "This definitely isn't how I'd been planning to spend my Valentine's Day," she said, as Tom slid a truffle onto her tongue. "But it's almost time for me to meet my friends."

"I haven't even given you your gift yet. Wait right there." Tom walked back to his storeroom and returned with a big wrapped present. He set it next to her in front of the huge storefront window, and the glow of the streetlamp illuminated the scene. It was a beautiful moment.

She clasped her hands together. "What is that? A foam cutter? A heat gun?"

He laughed. "Just open it."

She hesitated because the wrapping was so beautiful, but then she tore off the curly gold bows and the shiny red paper. "Oh, Tom!" It was a stool that matched her chair. "Where did you find this?"

"When I saw your chair, I remembered a guy I'd bought some antiques from downtown. I was sure he had one of these, and I hadn't taken it because it was a mismatch to the chair he did have. I called him up and refinished it for you. Do you like it?"

She jumped up and hugged him. "I love it. It's the most thoughtful gift I've ever gotten."

"Good. You deserve something special like that." He bent down to kiss her, and she wrapped her arms around his neck. But then the room dimmed a bit, and she realized someone was standing in front of the window, watching.

"We've got an audience," she said, with a giggle.

"Who cares, we're two fools in love in Valentine's day."

She wasn't sure what shocked her more—the love part, or seeing Harper's stunned face in the window when she turned around.

They stared at each other for a moment, like two deer realizing they're about to get creamed by a semi. Lori was rounding up an explanation in her head, when she realized Harper was arm-in-arm with a very handsome man.

Harper dragged him inside the store. "Lori, what's going on here?"

Tom walked behind her and put his arms around her. "This is my upholstery teacher," Lori mumbled, heat blazing her cheeks.

Harper's mouth hung open. "You said he was old and cranky!"

Tom's arms dropped away. "You said I was old and cranky?"

"I lied!" Lori said.

"And you broke the resolution!" Harper said, sounding hurt.

"What resolution?" Tom's smile had disappeared.

"Her resolution—the one you made up, Lori! You didn't tell him?"

Lori took a deep breath. "My friends and I decided to give up guys for New Year's—just for a few weeks to focus on something else for a change. That's why I took your class. And I kept telling myself it was okay to go to dinner with you since were talking about upholstery stuff, or that stopping by your house would be like a field trip." She shrugged. "But I fell for you. And I totally broke the resolution."

Harper slapped her knee. "See, I told you we'd meet men—since we resolved not to—because resolutions never work."

"Yeah, what about you and the arm candy here," Lori asked. "Looks like I wasn't the only one who failed."

Harper tipped up her nose. "Believe it or not, he's in my belly dancing class, and we have not kissed, we're waiting until tonight when the resolution is up." She jabbed her thumb against her chest. "I followed the rules."

Patrick cleared his throat. "Actually, I did kiss you that one time when we stayed after class."

She whacked him with her purse. "Right, but we haven't been having passionate interludes like these two."

Lori checked her watch. "We're supposed to meet Claire at the bar in half an hour. You guys might as well come along when we 'fess up to her."

"She's going to kill us," Harper whispered.

"No, she'll just pout and rub it in for a few weeks," Lori said. "I hope."

They drove to the bar, ready for the wrath of Claire. They'd never hear the end of it from her. She'd been taking scuba lessons from an angry old Navy SEAL, no chance she'd been going out with him.

They stood outside the bar for a moment, until the cold got the better of them. "We're early," Harper said. "We shouldn't be nervous to go in. She's not here yet."

But still, they stood there as their toes froze in their totally-inappropriate-for-the-weather pumps. "Let's get it over with," Lori said, stomping her feet and pushing open the door.

***

Claire couldn't stand it any longer. "Nate, it's Valentine's Day. The resolution is over. Kiss me already."

"Not until my shift is done." He set another drink in front of her. "A kiss-tini."

She pushed it away. "I want a real one, before my friends get here." She was sitting on the side end of the bar and snuck a peek at the door. They wouldn't be here for at least twenty minutes. Standing up on the rungs of the stool, she leaned over the side of the bar, grabbed Nate by his tie, and pulled him to her. She set her hands on the side of his face and gave him the kiss she'd been dreaming about for weeks.

When they came up for air, he said, "Maybe I can take a ten-minute break out in my car."

While Claire waited for him to duck from behind the bar, she turned to the door and saw Harper and Lori with their arms crossed and toes tapping. Harper pointed at her. "You were canoodling!"

Claire's heart started racing. "That's the first time we've kissed! I've been coming here on Thursday nights and we've just been talking."

"I thought you were taking scuba lessons on Thursdays."

Claire bit her lip. "I kind of flunked out. I couldn't swim the whole length of the pool. I was nursing my blues here at the bar. But I didn't break the resolution." That's when she noticed the two men standing by her friends. "What the hell is this?"

Lori jerked her thumb at Tom. "Hot reupholstering teacher."

Harper wrapped her arm around Patrick. "Hot belly dancing student. He's her first male student ever. Imagine that?"

They all stood there, silently staring at each other, when Claire's phone rang. Grateful for the distraction, she answered it. "Oh, hey Ginny!" She listened for a moment, nodding and smiling, then turned to her friends. "Ginny's just calling to say Happy Valentine's to her single gal pals." Claire turned back to the phone. "The resolution? Yeah, that's over tonight. Um, it went really well. Mmm, hmm, it worked out just like we wanted." Claire held out the phone to the girls. "Say Happy Valentine's Day to Ginny, everybody, and tell her stop bragging about how warm it is down there."

"Happy Valentine's day!" the group said.

Claire put the phone back to her ear. "Guys? You heard guys? Sorry Ginny, the line's breaking up. I gotta go. Talk soon sweetie!"

She hung up and dropped the phone in her purse.

Patrick stepped forward and made a time out sign. "Okay, so does this mean the resolution is officially over?"

The girls looked at each, shrugged and nodded. "I guess so," Lori said.

"Good." Patrick took Harper in his arms, and dipped her, giving her a long, end-of-the-war kind of kiss.

That got some hooting and hollering from folks in the bar.

"Get a room!" someone shouted.

Harper came up for air and looked to see who said it. She clapped her hand over her mouth. "It's the canoodlers! From New Year's!"

The girl wiggled her fingers at them in a friendly, but teasing wave.

Lori nudged Claire. "Look, she's got an engagement ring now!"

The door to the bar burst open and a man and woman walked in. "Can I have your attention please? For those of your dawdlers, those last minute shoppers or those who've just met the love of your life tonight, I've got good news. The Save Land mobile shopping van is outside with Valentine's day cards, chocolates, teddy bears, you name it. Come on out for a look."

The woman next to him was beaming. "That was my idea." She nodded. "He's lucky to have me."

"I sure am, Lindy."

People started heading for the door, and Nate was pulling Claire outside, too.

"You don't need to buy me a teddy bear," she said.

He looked at her funny. "I want my ten minute make-out session in the car."

She laughed and followed him.

"Wait!" Harper shouted. "We have to have another toast!"

Lori grabbed them flutes of champagne from a passing cocktail waitress. "To true love. May it always last!"

"Here, here!" said the group.

"Wait!" Harper said, lowering her drink. "Does this really mean we don't want it to last because resolutions never work?" She bit her lip and stared at the ceiling as she tried to work it out.

Patrick pulled her in his arms. "It's not a resolution, silly. It's a promise."

She looked at him with wide eyes. "Oh, that's much better than a resolution."

Lori raised her glass again, and canoodling couple from the bar even joined them. "To love!" she said.

"To love!" they all said.

"Okay, now we're getting the hell out of here, I've waited long enough for this," Patrick said, taking Harper by the hand.

He dashed to the door with three other couples close behind.

About The Author

Lisa Scott is a former news anchor who now makes up stories for a living. She's also a voice actor living in upstate New York with her kids, hubby, cats, dog, and koi fish. Check out her website, ReadLisaScott.com and sign up for her newsletter to be notified about new releases. Like her on facebook at Read Lisa Scott. Thanks for reading!

Lightning Source UK Ltd.
Milton Keynes UK
UKHW03f2111160418
321151UK00001B/179/P